THE DARINGS

OF THE RED ROSE

THE DARINGS
OF THE RED ROSE

By Margery Allingham

Introduction by B. A. Pike

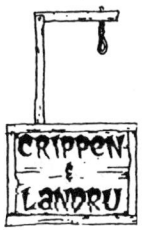

Crippen & Landru, Publishers   Norfolk, Virginia 1995

Copyright 1930 by Margery Allingham and *Weekly Welcome*
This Edition copyright © 1995 by P. and M. Youngman Carter Ltd.
Introduction copyright © 1995 by B. A. Pike
Cover and layout copyright © 1995 by Crippen & Landru, Publishers.

Cover by Deborah Miller
Crippen & Landru logo by Eric D. Greene

ISBN 1-885941-01-3

FIRST EDITION

Printed in the United States of America on acid-free paper

10 9 8 7 6 5 4 3 2 1

THE DARINGS

OF THE RED ROSE

CONTENTS

Introduction	9
Episode 1	21
Episode 2	41
Episode 3	55
Episode 4: The Lady at the Crossroads	71
Episode 5: The Girl on the Fire-Escape	87
Episode 6: The Watcher Behind the Curtain	103
Episode 7: The Whisper on the Phone	119
Episode 8: Her Day of Reckoning	135

[*Publisher's note: The first three stories do not have individual titles, and after 65 years it is too late to provide them.*]

INTRODUCTION

Of the two accounts of *The Darings of the Red Rose* in the secondary literature devoted to Margery Allingham, the first, by Youngman Carter, is vague and misleading. It occurs in his memoir of his wife, written as an introduction to an otherwise unremarkable volume called *Mr. Campion's Clowns*, published by Chatto & Windus in 1967. In discussing his wife's work for magazines in the earlier phase of her career, he referred to "an epic serial dealing with the adventures of The Society Millgirl and the Seven Wicked Millionaires."[1] This is *The Darings of the Red Rose*, actually a series of linked stories, eight, not seven, in number. The tantalising hint of an unknown early work was not taken up until Julia Thorogood, in the course of writing her biography of Margery Allingham,[2] came across the stories and went on to describe them in her book: "They detail the step-by-step revenge exacted, Robin-Hood style, by a beautiful, if mysterious, society girl on eight wicked financiers

---

[1] *Mr. Campion's Clowns*, p. 11. This omnibus contains "slightly abridged" versions of *Mystery Mile*, *Coroner's Pidgin* (*Pearls Before Swine*), and *More Work for the Undertaker*.

[2] *Margery Allingham: A Biography* (Heinemann, 1991).

INTRODUCTION

who have brought ruin on her family. She leaves a small rosebud as her trademark."[3]

The series was written for a women's magazine called *Weekly Welcome* and appeared in eight issues published between 15 February and 5 April 1930. Each story was illustrated but nowhere was the artist named; nor, indeed, was the author. From the fourth in the sequence the stories have individual titles, but the earlier three are not separately named. The magazine was published from Fetter Lane in London by D. C. Thomson Ltd., a Dundee firm for which Herbert Allingham, Margery's father, also wrote stories and serials. Both Herbert and his wife Emily wrote magazine fiction and he in particular earned a reputation as one of the most resourceful and dependable writers in this field. Interestingly, Julia Thorogood records that both Margery's parents published stories about female detectives: he in "the Harmsworth market leader," *Puck*, and she in *Woman's Weekly* ("the exploits of Phinella Martin—'the beautiful and famous lady detective'").[4] Though the Red Rose is an avenger rather than a detective, her adventures continue an established family tradition.

In writing about her development as a mystery novelist,[5] Margery Allingham makes clear the distinction between her

---

[3] *Op. cit.*, p. 125.

[4] *Op. cit.*, p. 36.

[5] Preface to *Mr. Campion's Lady* (Chatto & Windus, 1965), p. 8. This omnibus contains *Sweet Danger*, *The Fashion in Shrouds*, *Traitor's Purse*, and a brief story "Word in Season," uncollected elsewhere. *The Fashion in Shrouds* is newly revised by the author.

INTRODUCTION

"left hand" and "right hand" writing, between that done purely from "commercial" considerations and that undertaken more "seriously," though also "for fun." She describes the right hand writing as "the story one tells spontaneously at a party " which involves "only oneself and the audience." It is essentially a "private" process and the author takes sole responsibility for what results. Left hand writing, however, is the story "one is made to tell by somebody else." The editor's role is crucial, so much so that all left hand work "could be signed 'Allingham with help.'"

The right hand work includes the novels on which Allingham's reputation rests: these she wanted to write and enjoyed writing. The left hand work began with non-stop hack journalism: film stories for *Girl's Cinema*, the "Little Scratches" for *Joy*, and "verse and occasional features" for *The Picture Show*.[6] Later, there were three serials for *Answers*, published in book form under the pseudonym "Maxwell March,"[7] the long story "The Mystery Man of Soho,"[8] the Red Rose sequence, and even the early Campion stories written for *The Strand*, with a high degree of right hand finish. By virtue of their similarity and separateness,

---

[6]*Margery Allingham: A Biography*, p. 112.

[7]*Other Man's Danger* (1933), *Rogues' Holiday* (1935), and *The Shadow in the House* (1936). In *Answers*, the serialisations were in Margery Allingham's name. *Other Man's Danger* appeared as *Dangerous Secrets* and *The Shadow in the House* as *The Devil and Her Son*.

[8]This story is collected in *The Allingham Minibus* (Chatto & Windus, 1973) as "A Quarter of a Million."

INTRODUCTION

the four post-war novellas[9] might also be considered left hand products, except that Julia Thorogood gives no indication of editorial intervention.

Weekly Welcome was emphatically feminine and must have resembled *Joy*, a weekly founded by Margery's Aunt Maud and described by Julia Thorogood as "a magazine for the would-be 'flapper,' the typist or shop-girl who was eager to be up-to-date."[10] In *Weekly Welcome*, Hetty's "London Letter" offered "red-hot fashion news"[11] and Isabelle undertook to help readers "improve their good looks." Estelle Clare served as the magazine's "dress expert" and Martha dealt with problems of the heart in "Confidence Corner." Gifts were offered with each issue: "the Witches' Love Token" on 15 February, "the New Star Album of the Latest Talkies" on 22 February and a "Luck-stone Necklet" on 1 March. Married women were also addressed by the editor, who claimed unblushingly that "Mothers all over the country have found Nurse Edith Miles a real helpful friend when

---

[9]"Wanted: Someone Innocent" and "Last Act" were collected together as *Deadly Duo* (Doubleday, 1949; British title, *Take Two at Bedtime*, World's Work, 1950). "The Patient at Peacocks Hall" and "Safer than Love" were collected together as *No Love Lost* (World's Work, 1954). "Wanted: Someone Innocent" (along with three short stories) had previously appeared in the United States as *Wanted: Someone Innocent and Other Stories* in the short-lived Pony Books paperback series (Stamford House, 1946).

[10]*Margery Allingham: A Biography*, p. 111.

[11]All quotations from *Weekly Welcome* are from the issues featuring *The Darings of the Red Rose*, published between 15 February and 5 April, 1930.

INTRODUCTION

... worried about their little ones." Joe Neighbour offered gardening tips and Aunt Jane told cosy stories about dear, good, kind people, among them the "new neighbour who can Listen, Laugh and Shed a Tear." Serials included "Her Son Who Got On," "Her Stolen Bairn" ("being talked about all over the country") and the immediate successor to the Red Rose, "Famous Fascinators of Women." Best of all for the cynical modern reader is the home hints and cookery expert, whose name, Betty Martin, gives the whole show away.[12]

Margery Allingham was twenty-five when the Red Rose series was published, still a 'prentice novelist, though moving towards maturity with *Mystery Mile*, also published early in 1930. She would doubtless have been astonished to see her anonymous potboilers revived after sixty-five years, not least because they are so unmistakably left hand work, written to formula and limited by their original context. In *Mr. Campion's Lady*, she defines exactly her approach to such an assignment: "One must discipline the imagination and observe the rules and remember the idiosyncrasies and, above all, bow the knee" to "the perishable element," the "fashion of the day."[13]

The Red Rose sequence keeps the rules and must have pleased its contemporary readers greatly. It offers excitement and suspense but also romance and a strong appeal to the sympathies. The heroine carries all before her: with

---

[12] "All my eye and Betty Martin" is an outmoded colloquial phrase meaning "nonsense."

[13] *Mr. Campion's Lady*, p. 8.

INTRODUCTION

minor exceptions, the men are either ineffectual or hateful. The course of true love runs far from smoothly but all is well by the final embrace.

The stories conform to a pattern, each with an object that is achieved in the course of the action. The motive force for the series is revenge and we are continually reminded of the wrongs that have to be righted. The avenger is Betty Connolly, a society belle destined to marry into the aristocracy once her self-appointed task is done. She and her family were victims of a vast financial swindle, together with the rest of their home community. Now she seeks redress from the eight men responsible, determined that they shall pay back the money they stole.

Betty is a fantasy figure on an impressive scale, admirably drawn in an appropriately romantic manner and not without intensity. She is beautiful but enigmatic, a classic combination. Her lover, Tommy Kempis, is the younger son of an earl, handsome but dense and a dabbler in detection. Betty continues to bewilder and tantalise him until the end, but she does not for long remain mysterious to the reader. When we meet her she is already a woman with a past, in a distinct third stage of her life, having gone from riches to rags and back again. Her Cinderella phase over, she now models herself on Robin Hood. With no personal need of money from the swindlers, she contrives that they contribute heavily to a fund set up to rehabilitate the community they have destroyed.

Betty's extended revenge is complicated by Tommy's association with Scotland Yard, which involves her in a classic conflict of love and duty: as her maid observes, "It's a pity about Mr. Kempis . . . . It seems as if he's on the

INTRODUCTION

wrong side." He has some reputation with the official force and they are beginning to tip their helmets to him at the Yard. Despite this, the Red Rose case is one of his failures—not surprisingly, since he disregards all the signs of Betty's dual life, even those he notices. The convention, of course, demands that he fail: how else could Betty win through to the end? He might have discovered her secret and thrown in his lot with her, but that would have made a different story. At one point where it seems he must tumble to the truth, providence intervenes, in the approved manner. Throughout, Betty depends absolutely on her maid, Marie, invaluable both in herself and for the men at her command. Since Betty is unable to call on her own lover, she enlists the men attracted to Marie: Schuyler Krafft's butler, Henry, who contrives his master's social humiliation; and the young man Jack, who deals so capably with Theodore Windover. In the final episode, Betty's chauffeur Jim rallies to the cause.

The ranks of the enemy are daunting and might have appeared impregnable: Betty is not only Robin Hood but also Jack the Giant-killer. The succession of swindlers adds considerably to the interest of the stories: though stock figures they are far from lifeless. They tend to be overfed, with narrow eyes and cruel mouths. Specifically, Jonathan is big and brutal; Schrafft "bird-like" and "greedy"; Rodd "immense" and "formidable"; Benham mean and conceited; Capet flabby and frightened; Wild small and self-satisfied; Windover sadistic and "repulsive"; Drayton "hard" and "vindictive." Jonathan and Windover are particularly well drawn, the one "the chief vandal of all," the other "the man most deserving of punishment," for whom Betty reserves

INTRODUCTION

her most violent hatred. Besides their shared vanity, meanness and hypocrisy, each has a weak spot, which Betty exploits: Jonathan's obsession with his diamond, Krafft's dual identity, Benham's baby son, Drayton's fear of the police. When the tables are turned, they cave in completely, Jonathan screaming "like a maniac," Krafft "beyond self-control," Rodd "cringing, terrified," and Capet "shaking all over like a jelly." Even the sadistic Windover is reduced to pleading for his life.

The revenge pattern sustains the stories but also tests the author's capacity to vary the formula. It is a measure of her skill that, for the most part, she achieves this. Despite points of similarity between one episode and another, the handling ensures that we never feel we are reading the same story twice. Two jewel thefts are effectively diversified and parallel traps are sprung with clever variations in the treatment. Even the rehabilitation fund is repaid in different ways: by donation under pressure, by a private benefaction, by the generous charity of an altruistic young couple.

Their ephemeral nature is the stories' best defence against adverse criticism. They falter only on a searching analysis of the kind they were not intended to withstand. Nonetheless, there are irritants that might easily have been avoided and suggest that the left hand's "help" was insufficiently vigilant on occasion. There are infelicities of style and clumsy sentences.[14] Words are misused: "disinterestedness" for "want of interest" and "famous" to describe a

---

[14] E. g., "Luck was with her . . . .," below p. 31.

INTRODUCTION

secret notebook. In "The Girl on the Fire-Escape," a "heavy child" is exchanged for "a poor, fragile ... wasted" one, yet suddenly he is descibed as the "lighter bundle" of the two. Marie's admirer is insufficiently established and even undergoes a mid-stream name-change from Henry to Jack.

Improbabilities are par for the course in this kind of fiction, part of the thriller-writer's licence. Like all pulp heroines worthy of the name, Betty leads a charmed life and has phenomenal luck; and even when it runs out, circumstances combine to save her. As she moves in to steal the Jonathan diamond, the guards are distracted by an argument over their poor pay. When she needs to escape in an unfamiliar car she finds that "fortunately it was a make ... she knew." On recognising the pattern of the mechanism controlling Octavius Rodd's lift, she utters "a little sigh of relief"—as well she might, since her entire scheme depends on it. We are told that "her two faithful helpers had prepared a plan of [Benham's] house and grounds" but not how this remarkable feat was achieved. Most astonishing of all is her ability not only to abduct a sleeping baby via a fire-escape but to leave another in his place without either child waking and rousing the household.

None of this matters, of course: one submits with a willing suspension of disbelief or one reads something else. On their own terms, the stories succeed, and since they are the accomplished hack-work of a major detective novelist they continue to be of interest. The readers of *Weekly Welcome* would hardly have heard of the author even if the series had been attributed to her, but we have the advantage

INTRODUCTION

of hindsight and the temptation to look for hints and turns of phrase is irresistible in 1995.

How much of the familiar Allingham manner is apparent in *The Darings of the Red Rose*? Her narrative zest is assuredly in evidence and certain sentences catch and command the attention—"Her great grey eyes were dancing and her lips quivered with pleasure"; "I never saw such a brute of a man, hard as nails—oozing with money, and as mean as sin"; "It was a high, thin faraway voice, strangely weird and terrifying in that great empty building"—but it would be absurd to claim that such as these are clues to the author's identity. More persuasive are the accounts of Betty's wardrobe, from her first appearance in a "diaphanous white gown, which billowed out round her slender form from the long and tight fashionable corsage" to her last in a "sleeveless frock of almost green silk." Everything she wears is meticulously, even lovingly, described, with an exquisite precision that prefigures all the feminine fuss and flurry of the house of Papendeik, the glamour and chic of Val and Georgia, of Gina and Meg.[15] Her "frivolous little bag of silk and ostrich feathers" is a forerunner of other fashionable fripperies in the novels to come; and the "soft grey velvet upholstery" of her limousine is an eerie foreshadowing of Val's "famous grey Daimler" with its "soft,

---

[15] Val and Georgia are in *The Fashion in Shrouds*, as is the house of Papendeik. Gina is in *Flowers for the Judge* and Meg in *The Tiger in the Smoke*.

INTRODUCTION

grey-quilted depths . . . like a powder-closet . . . as exquisitely feminine as a sedan-chair."[16]

There is even an early-Allingham joke on occasion, as when Betty remarks that "everything hangs on that" in the Krafft episode or when she explains in the Rodd story that she is late because she has "had to give someone a lift." Tommy Kempis's name is also characteristic Allingham: a mischievous borrowing from a venerable sage far removed from him in time and temperament.

Margery Allingham suppressed *The White Cottage Mystery*[17] during her lifetime and it is unlikely that she would have wanted to revive the Red Rose, but the stories do her no disservice and should even add to her reputation: not because they are undiscovered masterpieces but because they demonstrate so forcibly that she was a truly professional writer who could turn her hand to anything.

B. A. Pike
London
December 1994

---

[16] *The Fashion in Shrouds* (Heinemann, 1938), p. 312.

[17] *The White Cottage Mystery* (Jarrolds, 1928) is Margery Allingham's first crime novel, preceding Albert Campion's first appearance.

EPISODE 1

"Miss Connolly will be down in one moment, sir, if you don't mind waiting."

The dainty parlour maid closed the door behind her, and the Honourable Tommy Kempis was left alone in the softly lit, luxuriously furnished drawing-room. The curtains were drawn, shutting out the soft rumble of traffic in the Mayfair street without. The gilt ormulu clock at the other end of the room proclaimed the hour to be half-past eight.

Thomas Kempis sat down on a little Louis XV settee, which was placed to one side of the fireplace, where a fire blazed in spite of the earliness of the season, and spread out his long thin legs to the heat. He was a handsome young man not yet thirty, immaculately dressed in the most faultless of evening clothes. He took out a narrow silver case from his pocket and selected himself a cigarette which he lit and began to smoke, still staring into the fire, a faint smile of satisfaction on his wide sensitive mouth.

He was thinking of Betty Connolly, the girl he had come to see; the girl who was at once perhaps the most popular and mysterious of women in all social London. No one knew much about her. She had been left a fortune from some distant relation in America, that much everybody knew.

Even to himself, perhaps one of her closest friends, Betty had never spoken about her life before she came to London. She had been sponsored into the exclusive circles of society by old Lady Derry, but that silent and austere old aristocrat was not at all the type to gossip about her protégées. Apart from a vague idea that beautiful Betty Connolly came "from the North" no one knew anything at all about her.

Thomas Kempis was not curious on this point. During the months that he had known the girl she had become a part of his life, so much so that his only interest was in herself, her thoughts and her affections. Still, he reflected to himself, there was something curious about her, a strange sadness, which seemed to seize her at times, a curious rebellious expression which appeared in her eyes at moments when it was least expected.

Meanwhile, upstairs in her luxurious boudoir, beautiful Betty Connolly sat at her dressing-table, her lovely head bowed over a little crimson note-book; the curious expression which Kempis had noticed was once again in her eyes. She was quite alone. Her maid had already gone downstairs, and although she knew that her escort was waiting, she still lingered over the little book.

Anyone looking in upon her would not have found it difficult to understand why she had taken London by storm. She was not tall but inexpressibly slender, with a perfect figure, sleek dark hair which waved smoothly down either side of her pale oval face into a soft fashionable knot at the nape of her neck. Her eyes were blue and very clear. Hers was a typical Lancashire loveliness.

THE DARINGS OF THE RED ROSE

Lancashire. That was the true explanation of the mysterious expression which now saddened her face.

Before she had come to London only a few short months ago, she had been a penniless workgirl in Manchester. But it had not always been thus. Betty had been born into an old North-country family known and respected for hundreds of years in the little village of Wellside, near Manchester. And then suddenly when she was eighteen years old a calamity had overtaken not only her own family, but all the wealthy, simple, home-loving folk in her district. The girl's eyes hardened as she looked down at the page of the little note-book.

On it there were written eight names, each one of them famous over half the world as representative of large fortunes.

These were the names of eight members of the same syndicate, that syndicate which, while keeping within the law, had brought Betty's own folk to degradation, poverty, and in the case of her own father and mother, to death.

When the unexpected legacy from an American relative had made her ambition possible, she had seized it, and come to London. For she had pledged herself to make them pay, these eight. She had made up her mind that each one of them should be made to suffer for the incomparable wrongs they had done.

The first name of the list in the little book was Barnaby Jonathan, the Chairman of the Syndicate, chief vandal of them all. Betty laughed to herself, and her little gold pencil hovered over the name.

"Perhaps," she said softly, "perhaps quite soon I shall be able to write 'paid' to your name, Mr. Jonathan. I hope you got my note."

Then slipping the book into the dressing-table drawer, she locked it, and taking up a small crimson flower from a silver vase on the table, she slipped it into her bag and went downstairs to the drawing-room.

She stood for a moment in the doorway smiling in at Tommy, while the young man stared at her in rapt admiration. She was radiant; he had never seen her look so lovely. No one would have dreamed that behind her smiling eyes there glowed fiercely the bitter fire of revenge.

"Tommy, you're a darling to come for me," she said, holding out her hands to him. "It's ever so good of you to take me, too. I'm tremendously grateful."

He stood looking at her without speaking as if her loveliness had rendered him dumb for the time being. She met his gaze, and a faint flush tinted her pale cheeks.

"You're admiring my frock," she said hastily. "It is rather nice, isn't it?"

She shook out the folds of her diaphanous white gown, which billowed out round her slender form from the long tight fashionable corsage.

"Beautiful," said the young man gravely, but it was not at the dress that he stared.

"I'm afraid you're going to be terribly bored," she went on lightly, slipping on the soft grey squirrel cloak which her maid now held up to her. "But do you know, as soon as I saw that invitation I simply couldn't resist the idea of going. 'The Seven Stars' diamond, doesn't that sound romantic?"

THE DARINGS OF THE RED ROSE

Her laughter was infectious, and he joined in with her.

"As a matter of fact," he said as they wandered through the hall to the waiting limousine which was to take them to their destination, "I should have gone to Mr. Jonathan's party to-night in any case." The contempt with which he spoke the name was not lost upon the girl. She glanced at him quickly.

"You dislike him?" she said.

Her companion shrugged his broad shoulders. "Naturally," he said, "there's not much to like about him, is there? It's not that I'm particularly snobbish," he went on, eager to vindicate himself, "it's the fearful stories about him in the city. He came from the North originally, I believe, and—"

"I know. Manchester way." It was the girl's voice which had interrupted him. They had entered the car by this time, and he turned to her curiously as she sat beside him on the soft grey velvet upholstery. Her voice had startled him, her expression bewildered him still more. Once again he caught a glimpse of the bitter sorrow in her face, that savage rebellion in her beautiful eyes.

She caught him staring at her and laughed to hide her embarrassment.

"That type of man always infuriates me," she said, "a man who has made his money out of the sufferings of others, a man whose beautiful mansion is built on the wreckage of a thousand little homes."

Kempis was surprised. He had seldom heard anyone speak with such feeling on a subject in which they were not personally involved. This remarkable girl became more mysterious and extraordinary every time he saw her. It was she who broke the silence.

"You said you would have come in any case," she said. "Why? Have you been bitten with the diamond fever also?"

He shook his head. "No, it's more serious than that," he said. "I don't know if you realise it, but old Jonathan is doing a pretty dangerous thing in showing that jewel to everybody to-night. There's no diamond like 'The Seven Stars' in the world. It's virtually priceless, but Jonathan gave three-quarters of a million for it—half his fortune, people say.

"It appears that it has always been the old man's ambition to own this particular stone. Some people are crazy about their possessions, but this man is stark staring mad about his. He idolizes it. It has become a fetish with him. It means more to him than anything else in the world, and to gain possession of it he has sacrificed everything, his wife, his children, his employees, they have all had to stand aside while he went on piling up gold in order to buy this stone."

His companion nodded. "Horrible, isn't it? A man like that ought to be made to suffer for the incredible evil he's done in the world. But that doesn't explain, Tommy dear, why you had to come anyway. I thought it was only out of kindness to me that you were deigning to join in the throng."

The young man looked at her helplessly. "You always laugh at me when I talk to you about my sleuthing activities."

THE DARINGS OF THE RED ROSE

A faint smile spread over her face. "It's my plebeian mind," she said. "The idea of the younger son of an Earl crawling about after crooks with a pair of handcuffs in one hand and a magnifying glass in the other always strikes me as being just a teeny-weeny bit comic. It's my appalling upbringing, I suppose. Still," she went on, laying a hand upon his arm, "I really am sympathetic in my heart. I know you've had wonderful successes already, and that Scotland Yard is beginning to touch its helmet when you go by. Do let me in on this secret. What's it all about? Surely Tommy," she clasped her hands in mock horror, "'The Seven Stars' hasn't been stolen before I've seen it?"

The man shook his head, and the little electric light with which the inside of the big car was illumined showed his handsome face to be dark and worried.

"Not yet," he said. "As a matter of fact my friend Downham of the Yard came to see me this morning. This is absolutely between ourselves, of course. I don't suppose you remember it, but I was able to give him a good deal of help last autumn in the Eldorado Case. He's not forgotten it, and this morning, as I said, he came to see me. Apparently old Jonathan has done some very shady work in his time, and his enemies are after him. Anyhow, this is the thing that terrified Jonathan."

And even while he wondered at himself for taking this girl so much into his confidence, even although she was such an old friend, he thrust his hand into his waistcoat pocket and drew out a folded scrap of notepaper which had struck such fear into Barnaby Jonathan, millionaire, only that morning.

He handed it to Betty, who spread it out. It was a thick sheet of hand-made paper, exquisitely perfumed, and on it written in a clear round hand had these few lines: "You will know the meaning of the Red Rose by midnight. There is someone who has not forgotten Wellside."

The girl raised her eyes. Her heart was beating furiously, but she did not betray her agitation.

"Is that all?" she said.

Kempis nodded. "Save that a small crimson rosebud was folded in the paper there was no other explanation of any sort."

"I see," said Betty quietly. "And what was 'Wellside'?"

The man smiled. "That's what a lot of people would like to know. Old Jonathan swore he'd never heard of the place before, but Downham had an idea that he remembered a scandal connected with Jonathan over some rather fishy business concerning the village of Wellside in Lancashire."

A faint smile appeared upon the girl's lips, and she turned her head away, but although he could not see her face, Kempis had the uncomfortable feeling that that same rebellious expression that he had noticed in her before had again come into her eyes.

The First Red Rose

Mr. Barnaby Jonathan stood in his vast drawing-room looking, as somebody rudely remarked, like a pig in a golden sty. Certainly, whatever his wealth had purchased for Mr. Jonathan, it had not brought him beauty. He was a heavy, unprepossessing man nearing fifty. All the arts of

THE DARINGS OF THE RED ROSE

Savile Row had been unable to lend his vast form any suggestion of the waist he so patently desired. His large red face, surrounded by a circle of superfluous flesh, could never at any time have been handsome. He had small dark eyes, which sparkled and twinkled greedily as he looked about him. But by far the most unattractive feature of this unprepossessing face was the mouth, small, cruel, and pursed like a string-bag.

A glittering crowd filled the drawing-room, although only a sprinkling of society folk had come. Only those who were interested in any new fad, however ridiculous, had accepted Mr. Jonathan's invitation, solely because they wished to see the famous diamond which had only lately come to England from one of the national treasure houses of Europe.

"I say, this place is getting on my nerves," whispered Kempis to Betty. The two had just entered and stood on the outskirts of the little crowd, wondering how best to make their way to the host through the throng.

She laughed softly. "Never mind. You may be able to catch the Red Rose," she whispered.

Kempis glanced round him anxiously, but no one was in earshot. "I assure you it's no joking matter, Betty. Anyway, old Jonathan doesn't seem to think so."

The girl followed the direction of his eyes and saw that the big heavy man at the far end of the room was glancing about him nervously, and in his small black eyes there was fear besides greed.

Suddenly he caught sight of the two and came forward eagerly.

"I'm so glad you have come to see my diamond." The financier bent forward without releasing the girl's hand from his flabby grasp. "It's in the next room. I have to be careful, very careful." Once again he looked behind him with a peculiarly jerky movement of his head which betrayed his apprehension for his treasure. "I have two detectives on guard day and night, but I have arranged a very pretty device for its safety. The key of the showcase in which it is displayed is here in my pocket." He tapped his waistcoat contentedly.

He glanced at his watch, a massive gold affair, chased and engraved with a thousand different designs. "It is nearly nine o'clock. At five minutes past I shall take you all in and you will have the honour of seeing the most wonderful jewel in the history of man."

To Kempis's astonishment Betty held out her hand.

"I hope you won't think I'm awfully rude," she said, smiling at the financier, "but may I look at your watch? I've never seen anything so wonderful."

Jonathan was only too delighted to show any of his treasures.

"Nice little thing, ain't it?" he said, dropping the incredible thing into her hand.

Betty turned it over. "Isn't it marvellous?" she said, turning to Kempis.

"Why—er—oh, yes, quite," he said dully, wondering at the same time whether she had taken leave of her senses.

"May I?" she said suddenly, and turning, slipped the watch into one of the man's waistcoat pockets. Mr. Jonathan laughed. "Not that one," he said, with an elephantine playfulness.

THE DARINGS OF THE RED ROSE

"How stupid of me." Kempis could hardly believe his ears. Betty was actually laughing with this man, she who had professed to dislike him so much. The young man was bewildered, and would have carried off his companion to demand an explanation when a footman appeared at Betty's elbow.

"Miss Connolly? You're wanted on the telephone, madam."

Betty raised her eyebrows. "How absurd," she said, and added, turning to the young man, "excuse me a moment. I can't imagine what it can possibly be."

The manservant conducted Betty into the large library where the telephone stood upon the desk. He indicated the instrument, and then went out, closing the door behind him, and the girl realised with a little thrill of satisfaction that he expected her to find her own way back. She took up the telephone and spoke softly.

"Thank you, Marie," she said to the maid who had 'phoned her. "You have done just what I told you. Goodbye."

Then she hung up the receiver and moved noiselessly towards the door. She opened it and peered out. Luck was with her: there was not a soul in the corridor, and directly opposite her was the door which the plan of the house which she had obtained beforehand from her lady's-maid, who had once been employed there, told her was that of the inner drawing-room, the room where the jewel was displayed. She unfolded her handkerchief and took from it the little key of the show-case which she had taken from Jonathan as she replaced his watch. It had been a dangerous thing to do, but she was not considering danger just then.

Still holding the key with her handkerchief to avoid all chance of finger-prints being left on the steel, she advanced cautiously towards the second door. Very carefully she turned the handle, using a panel of her dress to cover her hand, once again to avoid the tell-tale prints.

It was unlocked, and it swung open silently. As she peered into the room Betty held her breath. At first she could hardly believe her good fortune. She had come straight into the presence of the showcase door. The massive steel and glass safe was standing with its back to her between two heavy screens, which shut off all the other half of the room.

From behind the screens came the sound of low voices, angry voices. Betty stood listening, her heart thumping so loudly that she felt its very sound would betray her. Quickly she realised what was happening. There were two men on the other side of the screens, detectives. They were arguing fiercely between themselves over the inadequate gratuity given them by Jonathan. The front of the showcase, which was glass to display the Seven Stars, was covered with a black curtain which Barnaby Jonathan had arranged so that he could flick it aside at the appropriate moment and display his treasure to his guests.

In their preoccupation with their own affairs the detectives had not noticed the silent opening of the door. Betty knew that her one chance was to act, and to act quickly. Darting forward noiselessly, she slipped the key into the lock of the case, turned it silently, thrust in her hand, and, her pale fingers closing over the great jewel, she drew it forth. Then, quick as lightning, she placed the rosebud which she had brought with her in its place, closed the safe door, relocked it, and slipped like a shadow from the room.

Once back in the library she found that she was trembling. The actual substitution had been so swiftly done that she had not had time to be frightened, but now that she stood in the library with the great glittering stone in her hand, she was desperately afraid. She pulled herself together valiantly, however.

Quick as lightning she opened her frivolous little bag of silk and ostrich feathers, and took out a large ornamental box of face powder. With fingers now steady she carefully raised the lid and buried the Seven Stars in the soft cream powder, smoothing the surface down again, so that the jewel was completely hidden. Then she replaced the top of the box, slipped it back in her bag, and deliberately left the frivolous little thing upon the desk by the telephone. Then, gripping the key of the safe in her handkerchief she deliberately walked back to the drawing-room.

The whole incident had taken less than five minutes.

Tommy was waiting for her by the door. The financier was still talking to the young man, and they both turned eagerly as Betty appeared.

"My message was nothing at all," she said as she came up. "My absurd maid rang me up to tell me that I'd forgotten to put on my necklace in case I should fancy that I'd lost it. These girls are almost too thoughtful."

She was still standing on the polished parquet floor which skirted the luxurious pile carpet. As she stepped on to it she seemed to catch the toe of her delicate white satin slipper under the edge of the pile. She stumbled forward, and was saved from falling by Barnaby Jonathan, who caught her in his arms. She remained there only the fraction of a second, but long enough to slip the key back in his pocket. The next moment she was laughing in apparent confusion.

"How clumsy of me," she said.

Jonathan was all compassion.

"Miss Connolly, you're trembling," he said. "It might have been a very nasty fall."

His familiar tone exasperated Thomas, who linked the girl's arm through his own.

"I'll take care of you now," he said, and Betty, with a feeling of relief at her heart, realised that he had not guessed for an instant that her fall had not been purely accidental.

Meanwhile, Barnaby Jonathan, who was followed by his guests, was advancing upon the great double doors which led into the inner sanctum where the jewel had been on display.

There were signs of suppressed excitement on all sides. There is something about a famous jewel which sheds a glamour quite different from anything else in the world. Betty took a deep breath. For the first time she saw the room from the front.

Barnaby Jonathan had something of a showman in his make-up. He had arranged the display of his treasure with the utmost care. Upon either side of the large steel showcase, standing with their backs to the screens, stood the two plain-clothes detectives, quiet now, and standing at attention, quite unaware of what had happened only five minutes before.

The plate-glass front of the case was still shrouded by the small black curtains which Jonathan proposed to switch aside at the right moment, to reveal his treasure to his friends.

"Now," he said, his voice trembling with ecstasy, "look!" With a single sweep of his hand he drew back the curtain, and the showcase and its contents came into view.

For a moment there was dead silence, then a faint titter of hysterical laughter flickered through the crowd. It was silenced immediately, however, by a howl of mingled rage and horror which echoed wildly through the room. All eyes were turned upon the financier. He was standing hunched up, his face thrust forward, and an indescribable expression upon his bulbous face.

Kempis seized Betty's arm. "Good heavens!" he whispered. "Look!"

The great showcase was empty, and lying upon the velvet cushion where the giant diamond once had been was a tiny red rosebud.

Jonathan swung round upon his guests and screamed at them like a maniac.

"No one leaves this room!" he shouted wildly. "I'll have you all searched; I'll have you all searched!"

A Debt Paid

It was two hours later when an angry group of well-dressed men and women filed out of Mr. Jonathan's ornate mansion. Their host was lying upstairs being attended by a doctor. A highly apologetic group of police officials had carried out Mr. Jonathan's threat. Since he had insisted upon it, every person in the house had been searched. Nothing had been found, and the indignation was unanimous.

Betty, standing on the bottom flight of steps in the front hall, turned to her companion, who, as a privileged person, had been allowed by the police to make his own investigations.

"What do you make of it, Tommy?" she said.

He shook his head. "It's astounding," he said. "The thing was done from behind. Someone must have got a duplicate key to the lock of the safe which opened at the back. Whoever did it crept into the room not five minutes before old Jonathan exposed the glass, for the plain-clothes men are certain that they lifted the curtain at nine o'clock precisely and the jewel was there then." He paused and stared at her. "Isn't it extraordinary? It was quite easy to get into the room of course, but almost incredible to believe that someone slipped in there, just behind the safe, unfastened the door with a duplicate key, put the rose in its place, removed the jewel, and then vanished. There are no finger-prints—nothing. It looks like magic to me."

Betty's blue eyes widened.

"How extraordinary," she said. "Let's get out of this. And yet— oh, Tommy!"

The annoyance in her face and voice was a perfect piece of acting.

"Don't think I'm an awful fool, but I've left my bag behind. I'll go back for it."

THE DARINGS OF THE RED ROSE

"Nonsense." He spoke authoritatively. "I'll get it. Where is it?"

Just for a moment her heart failed her. If she should be found out now, who would believe her if she told them of her real reason for taking the Seven Stars? But Tommy was waiting.

"Where is it, dear? I'll get it," he said.

Glancing into his face Betty knew that so far at any rate he had not suspected her.

"It's on the library table by the telephone. I left it there when I 'phoned," she said, keeping her tone careless with a great effort. "But I'd rather go myself, dear."

"Nonsense." He was off in a moment. She stood waiting for him, her heart thrashing against her side. It seemed ages before he returned, but he came at last, swinging the frivolous little thing from its slender handle.

"Infernal cheek," he said. "There was a policeman on guard against the library door, and although I explained he wouldn't let me bring it until he had opened it."

Betty felt that she was going to faint. Then, as if from a long way off, she heard his voice continuing.

"Of course when the idiot saw there was nothing but a powder box, which he opened, and lip-stick and a few shillings inside, he was tremendously apologetic. I was furious though."

Betty climbed into the car, and taking the bag shut the door.

"Tommy, you're a darling," she said, smiling up at him. "But—but you're not going to see me home this evening because I'm desperately tired."

Then she leaned back against the soft upholstery and closed her eyes. The danger was past, and Tommy, her dear detective Tommy, had never dreamed of suspecting her for an instant.

The Honourable Thomas Kempis stood looking after the disappearing car, his face dark with disappointment. He had not taken his dismissal with very good grace, and finally hailed a taxi, and went off to his club in the worst of tempers. He did not call upon Betty Connolly for almost a week just to show his resentment at her treatment of him. But at length he could keep away no longer, and calling upon her one morning was shown up to her boudoir where she sat in the most frivolous of crepe-de-chine suits, reading the newspapers.

Kempis glanced over her shoulder. "Hello," he said, "what's more interesting than I am that you'd rather read than welcome me?"

She smiled up at him over her shoulder. "Someone giving money away," she said. "Look!"

Kempis read the column she indicated.

"Immense Sum Given to the Poor of Stricken Lancashire Village," ran the headline, and underneath, "Mysterious Giver Refuses Identity." "The crowded village of Wellside, Lancs., has been overjoyed by the mysterious gift of an immense sum to aid its well-nigh starving inhabitants. It may be remembered that some years ago during a financial crisis several thousand Wellside investors lost all they had."

"Jonathan was mixed up in that crisis," said Betty. "Serves him right he lost his diamond, don't you think?"

THE DARINGS OF THE RED ROSE

"Eh—oh, yes, rather, anything you like," said Kempis absently. He was not thinking of Jonathan just then. He took a deep breath, and began to speak jerkily.

"Betty, all this week I've been sulking, and yet now I—I just felt I had to come and see you because—" He broke off. She had risen to her feet, and stood looking at him with grave anxious eyes.

"Tommy, darling," she said slowly, "don't—don't ask me now, please, because—"

The old haunting sadness returned to her face. "I've got something to do first, something I can't tell anyone about, not even you, an oath I've got to fulfil. Until that's done I can't promise anything, and oh, Tommy dear, I do want to so much."

The Honourable Thomas Kempis walked out of the boudoir, his heart beating rapidly. He had taken his dismissal more calmly this time. There was, he saw, a chance for him. Wild thoughts were surging through his head. There could be no doubt of Betty's sincerity when she had spoken of the pledge to which she was bound, the self-allotted task which she must accomplish before she even thought of herself.

At the very moment that he descended the stairs, Betty Connolly opened a drawer in her dressing-table, and from it removed her jealously-guarded little red notebook. Deliberately she took the gold pencil from its slot, and with shining eyes and lips parted, printed the word "Paid" after Barnaby Jonathan's name.

EPISODE 2

"Betty, you look more wonderful than ever!"

The Honourable Tommy Kempis presented himself, in a Savile Row suit, before one of the luxurious couches in the foyer of the Savoy and smiled down at the beautiful girl before him.

Betty Connolly, the girl about whom there were more conjectures, more admiring whispers, than any other in London's society, smiled at the newcomer reprovingly.

"You're late," she said. "Two whole minutes."

"I'm sorry," the young man protested. "My chauffeur got held up in a traffic jam. Please forgive me and come in and have tea."

She rose gracefully and stood beside him, an entrancing slender figure in a marvellous gown of powder blue satin under one of the new three-quarter length squirrel coats. As they walked down the steps to the huge sunken tea lounge where a famous orchestra was playing and the oval dance floor was already crowded, Betty turned to her companion and spoke lightly.

"Do tell me about your detective activities, Tommy," she said. "Have you discovered who the Red Rose is yet?"

Her tone was a masterpiece of carelessness, and no one would have guessed from it the personal interest which lay behind the words, least of all Tommy Kempis, who glanced about him nervously.

"My dear," he said, half under his breath, "do be careful. The police have a suspicion that this—er—person, whoever he or she is, is someone in our own set, and once the guilty person guesses that I am working on the case, any chance I may have of taking them unawares will be ruined."

He steered her to a table and they sat down. There was no one within earshot, and quite unbidden by Betty, the young man continued to talk about the mystery which had been intriguing all London for the past month.

"As a matter of fact, I'm rather worried," he said. "It isn't as if it was just a case of a single jewel robbery. The police are so afraid that the Red Rose has not finished yet."

"Why?" Betty opened her eyes wide in what was, to all appearances, innocent astonishment. "Have they heard from the mysterious person again?"

Tommy Kempis hesitated. The impulse to confide in this girl was very strong. He looked at her dubiously. Just for a moment she was taken off her guard, and in her eyes was that mysterious expression which had so often puzzled him.

Suddenly he succumbed to the temptation.

"Of course," he said, "it may be a hoax, but this morning the police received a message from old Schuyler Krafft, the financier. He is in an awful funk. I was talking to Gray, of the Yard, and he said he was positively ashamed of the man, he was in such an abject state when they interviewed him. And all because he received a letter this morning containing a red rose and a single sheet of paper with the words, 'How about Wellside?' written on it. He's

THE DARINGS OF THE RED ROSE

got an absurd armed guard round his house in Stanhope Street."

Betty shot him a shrewd glance. She could not help imagining the horror that would have appeared upon his young handsome face had he known that the author of the letter which so terrified Schuyler Krafft was taking tea by his side.

"Wellside?" she said casually. "Wasn't that the place that the Red Rose letters mentioned in the Barnaby Jonathan jewel robbery?"

Tommy nodded. "Yes, that's just what makes it so mysterious," he said. "You see, in Jonathan's case, the motive was quite reasonable. Jonathan had been one of the gang who had been responsible for the big crash there some years ago."

Betty sighed, and a bitter expression crept into her eyes.

"But in this case," Tommy went on, "it's much more extraordinary, because as far as we know, Krafft had nothing whatever to do with that affair. There were eight of them in it. Seven are still in London, and the eighth, a man called Jabez Blakeney, disappeared after serving a short term of imprisonment for wrongful conversion of funds in connection with some other company. It was thought at the time that he had gone to Canada. But I'm afraid I'm boring you," he broke off, noticing that the girl's glance had strayed off towards the dancing floor. She turned to him with a charming smile.

"Not at all, Tommy, I'm desperately interested. I was just watching that girl over there. Don't you think she has the most beautiful and tragic face you ever saw in your life?"

Tommy followed the direction of her eyes until his glance rested upon a pretty fair-haired girl whose wide blue eyes were filled with such an expression of misery that it was impossible not to recognise it. He turned to Betty.

"How extraordinary that she should be here," he said. "And with poor young Michael Wild too. You recognized them of course? Joan Krafft and Michael Wild."

Betty nodded. "Dreadfully tragic, isn't it? They're obviously so terribly in love, both of them, And he's so handsome, don't you think?"

Tommy looked critically at the handsome young giant dancing with the girl. "I suppose he is," he said. "How curious that we should see her just when we've been talking about her stepfather. I haven't got quite the rights of the story. What is it? Old Krafft won't agree to Joan marrying Michael on any account, they say. At last he's pulled off his lifetime's dream, he's got her engaged to the heir of a Duke—young Rochburg, as a matter of fact. That's it, isn't it?"

"Yes," said Betty quietly. "That's it. The engagement is not official yet, but I know I've received an invitation to a reception at Krafft's house, and I understand that he's going to make the announcement then."

"It's a shame," said Tommy hotly, whose interest in the dancing couple had revived. "I suppose they're having a sort of tragic farewell. Young Rochburg is such a dreadful specimen too. I can't understand any man preferring him to Michael, whatever title there was in the family."

Betty nodded. "I rather fancy there's more in it than that," she said. "Michael is by way of being a reformer. He has great ideas for helping the workers. I know he was particularly interested in those little places round Manchester—I believe Wellside was one of them. He has spent practically all his own fortune upon work of that sort, and old Krafft, who has spent all his life wresting his fortune from the poor, is very anxious that it should not return to them again."

Tommy smiled. "Quite likely," he said. "But, after all, he has a very good remedy against that. He needn't leave his daughter his money."

"I'm afraid that's no good," said Betty. "Krafft has been a little too clever. He has made over practically all his fortune to his daughter, to save death duties, and once she's married she can do practically what she likes with it."

Tommy chuckled. "Oh, I didn't know that," he said. "Rather an amusing situation, what? And yet, tragic for the girl," he added with sudden gravity, "especially when she's as much in love as that."

Betty nodded. "Tragic," she agreed, and there was real sympathy in her eyes as she looked at the little blonde. "All through an old man's wickedness," she said, "the needy lose a fortune and a beautiful girl the only man she ever loved. Someone ought to do something about that, Tommy."

"I know," the young man agreed sadly. "But it would take a miracle to set that right."

The old thoughtful look came into Betty's eyes.

"I wonder," she said softly.

MARGERY ALLINGHAM

The Schemer

Late that night, as Betty sat at her dressing-table, the secret drawer open at her side and the famous little notebook spread out upon the plate-glass surface of the table, there was an expression of intense excitement upon her beautiful face. Marie, the staunch North-country girl who had followed Betty to London from Wellside, and had adopted a French name and, occasionally, an accent, stood behind her friend and mistress, her quick dark eyes glowing with anticipation. The first of the eight names in the little book was neatly crossed off. The second name stood out at the two girls from the white paper—Jabez Blakeney, and in brackets, "Alias Schuyler Krafft."

There had been silence in the boudoir for some time, and now Betty broke it.

"I wonder how many people in London know that Schuyler Krafft and Jabez Blakeney are one and the same person?" she said.

Marie looked puzzled. "You say that Mr. Kempis didn't know," she said. "That seems rather strange. I thought the police knew everything."

Betty smiled faintly. "The police are very discreet," she said.

Marie nodded. "Perhaps so," she said. "But anyway I'll bet there's one person who doesn't know, and that's his Grace the Duke of Rochburg."

Betty shot her a swift, sidelong glance.

"Don't you be too sure, Marie," she said. "But there's one thing I'm banking upon. The Duke of Rochburg will never consent to his son marrying the daughter of a man who is known by everyone to have been in prison for fraud. And that's where we come in, lass. We're going to be Mr. Jabez Blakeney's publicity agents, and I rather fancy that incidentally we shall be playing fairy godmother to two very devoted young people, who will save us all the trouble of returning the so-called Mr. Krafft's vast fortune to the people to whom it really belongs. Now," she added briskly, "has my good friend in Paris sent us the precious sheet of paper yet?"

Marie nodded. "I have it here, Miss Betty," she said. "A special messenger brought it while you were out at tea to-day. It's exactly what we want, a photographic reproduction of the original placard with the lettering in French and English. It was pasted up in Boulogne just before our man was captured."

She moved quietly over to the big wardrobe as she spoke and took out a long cylinder of paper from one of the drawers. Betty pounced upon it eagerly, and for some time the two girls bent over the strange document that was to play such an important part in the history of the mysterious Red Rose.

"And now," said Betty, when she had satisfied herself that the document was all in order, "you know your part, Marie."

The girl smiled. "I've fixed it," she said. "Henry, Mr. Krafft's butler, will do anything for me. He has promised to show me over his master's house early to-morrow morning before the family are up. I know you don't approve of accomplices, but Henry is absolutely trustworthy. Besides," she laughed and blushed, "as I said, he'll do anything for me."

Betty passed her arm round the other girl's waist. "You're wonderful, Marie," she said. "Whatever should I do without you? I'll give you the red rose to-night," she went on. "That's very important. In fact, we might also say," she added, a little humorous smile appearing at the corners of her mouth, "that everything hangs on that."

Marie took her seriously. "That's true," she said. "Henry will fix that at the last moment. He's under notice to quit anyway, and he's very anxious to get his own back."

Betty smiled exultantly. "Who knows?" she said. "Perhaps to-morrow night I may able to put 'paid' to yet another account."

Marie looked at her mistress curiously. "Then," she said, a half-wistful, half-frightened expression in her eyes, "then—I don't know."

The Red Rose Strikes

The reception at Schuyler Krafft's house in Stanhope Street was crowded. Everyone knew that the engagement between Joan, the daughter of the house, and young Lord Dennis was to be officially announced, and the two young people were the centre of general interest. No one looking at Joan could possibly have imagined her to be happy. Her cheeks were pale, and she looked like some demure and tragic little ghost among the merrymakers.

Lord Dennis stood beside his father most of the time, and even the fine presence of the old aristocrat could not hide the glaring deficiencies of his heir.

THE DARINGS OF THE RED ROSE

Lord Dennis was a weakly, ineffectual-looking young man with lank yellow hair, and a general air of boredom that amounted almost to rudeness.

Betty, looking exquisitely lovely in a peach-coloured evening gown whose long graceful side panels suited her slender figure, glanced from the young nobleman to the girl with real pity in her eyes. Then her gaze wandered across the room to where the host of the evening stood talking arrogantly to a small group of society folk. He was a small, bird-like man, whose sallow face was set off by a great hooked nose and a pair of narrow, greedy eyes.

As Betty watched him, her lip curled and a wave of anger passed over her. When she recollected what this man and his confederates had done to her beloved home, she could hardly control her fury. She pulled herself together and a faint, half-humorous smile appeared upon her face. The time of her revenge and his humiliation was at hand.

It was at this moment that a well-known voice behind her made her turn, her hand outstretched. Tommy Kempis was standing looking at her, admiration in his eyes.

"I've been looking for you everywhere," he said. "I hate these crushes—I seem to meet everyone I don't want to, and to miss the one person in the place I'm anxious to see."

She smiled at him. "I'm glad you're here, Tommy. I didn't expect you," she said. "On business?" she added, half-laughing.

He frowned at her. "You're the most wonderful woman in the world and the most indiscreet one too," he said. "Come out of the crush. There's a fairly deserted spot over there by the palms."

Side by side they sauntered across the great glittering room with its blazing chandeliers and heavy gold-framed old paintings, until they reached the point of vantage that Tommy had indicated, a little apart from the rest of the crowd.

Betty's eyes wandered round the room with apparent casualness until her glance rested upon the old Duke of Rochburg, who had moved over to his host and was engaged in earnest conversation with him.

"Hullo," said Tommy. "The engagement is about to be announced. They're rather early."

Betty started imperceptibly at his side. If the engagement was indeed about to be announced at once, her plans had not been too well timed. But she was equal to any emergency. With what was apparently complete disinteredness in the "romance," she said casually, "Surely I saw that portrait in last year's Academy?"

Tommy followed her eyes to an oil painting on the panelling directly behind the spot where the master of the house stood.

Tommy nodded. "That's right," he said. "It's a portrait of Schuyler Krafft by a very famous painter. What do you think of it?"

"Not bad," said Betty judicially. "It flatters him a little, don't you think?"

Tommy laughed easily. "If it didn't," he said, "it would be unbearable. He's not a very pleasant-looking specimen, is he?"

He stood staring at the picture for some time until suddenly a little cry of astonishment escaped him and he

THE DARINGS OF THE RED ROSE

caught the girl's arm. "Betty," he said hoarsely, "do you see anything there?"

"Where?" said the girl, with a masterly imitation of indifference in her tone.

"There—on the picture cord above the frame. Look! A red rose!"

Betty was a born actress, and her start was the most natural thing in the world. A little stifled scream escaped her, and she threw out her hand. "A red rose," she said aloud.

Her cry reached the next group of people and the whisper passed on through the room.

Once the whisper got underway it was impossible to check it, and Tommy and Betty stood looking on, helpless to silence it if they would. At length it reached the two elderly men, so different in appearance and type, who stood talking with their backs to the picture.

The effect upon the financier was extraordinary. He spun round with a strangled cry of horror which reverberated throughout the astounded crowd. Then, dashing forward, he sprang up upon one of the little gilt chairs, and stretching out his hand tore down the flower to stamp it underfoot.

However, the moment his fingers touched the rose the thick cord which supported the picture suddenly snapped in his hands, and the heavy frame crashed to the ground with a noise that startled the whole room, and made even those in the further corners turn to stare.

Then came the great sensation of the evening. Marie had been as good as her word. Pasted upon the white panelling, pressed so tightly on that nothing short of hot water could ever remove it, was the sheet of paper over which the two girls had pored the night before. Now its purport was clear to everyone. It was a police "Wanted" notice, printed in both French and English, and by far the larger part of it was taken up by two portraits of the same man, one in profile, one in full face. The name below was Jabez Blakeney, but the face was the face of Schuyler Krafft.

Even then, perhaps, the man who now called himself Schuyler Krafft might have passed unrecognised as the one-time gaolbird and swindler, but, as he raised his eyes and suddenly came confronted with the poster, the iron nerve which had carried him through so many hazardous financial ventures suddenly gave way. A frenzied scream escaped him, and he began to tear at the paper on the wall with his nails.

In the shocked silence that followed, the old Duke's horrified whisper could be heard clearly in the great room.

"For heaven's sake, pull yourself together, sir."

But Schuyler Krafft, or to call him by his real name, Jabez Blakeney, was beyond self-control.

"It's not true!" he shouted wildly. "It's not true! And it's all over and done with anyhow. Tear it down! Tear it down!"

Very slowly and deliberately, losing nothing of his innate dignity, the old Duke of Rochburg turned away from the man who was to have been his son's father-in-law, and linking his arm through Lord Dennis's, led him quietly from the room.

This departure brought the stupefied crowd back to its senses, and amid much whispering the fashionable gathering began to disperse. Joan Krafft had disappeared. She had

THE DARINGS OF THE RED ROSE

gone out of the room just before the incident had occurred and had mercifully been spared the spectacle of her stepfather's humiliation.

Betty touched Tommy's arm. "Take me away," she begged. "You can't do any good here, my dear."

The young man nodded. There was a bewildered expression upon his face. "It's astounding," he said slowly. "Frankly, Betty, I was never more amazed in my life. If the Red Rose is an ordinary criminal, what is the point of a coup like this? What good does it do the mysterious being anyhow?"

Betty shook her head. She did not feel inclined at that moment to enter into a discussion of the Red Rose with Tommy.

They parted on the steps of Lady Derry's house, where Betty was living, and the young man looked at the girl wistfully.

"I suppose now is hardly the time to ask you once again?" he began, but the girl shook her head as always.

"I'm sorry, Tommy dear," she said. "But not yet—not yet."

And once again the Honourable Thomas Kempis went home wondering.

Upstairs in her room Betty seized her maid's hands and shook them heartily. "Marie, you were wonderful!" she said. "The thing went off just as we had planned."

A broad smile spread over the other girl's face.

"I knew it would," she said. "Henry promised me I shouldn't be disappointed. He frayed the picture cord himself this morning and he reckoned the lightest touch would bring the whole thing down immediately."

Betty smiled. "He was right," she said. "I never heard such a crash in my life. I was almost sorry for the man."

Marie shook her head and a steely look came into her black eyes. "Never," she said. "When you think of all the harm he's done, Miss Betty, all the misery he's caused, it is impossible to feel sorry. Besides, wasn't he about to make his daughter unhappy for life just because he wanted to have a title in the family?"

Betty nodded: all her old determination had returned.

It was not until some time later that the second name in the little book was crossed off. But one morning Marie brought up a letter to Betty, who was propped up among her pillows drinking her early cup of tea.

"Darling Betty," it ran. "I can't tell you how happy I am. Michael and I were married by special licence yesterday, and we are now staying in this tiny village and making the most wonderful plans for Michael's work among the poor.

"After the dreadful affair in Stanhope Street and the stories in the newspapers next morning, the Duke wouldn't hear any more of my engagement to Dennis. I was free! Oh, Betty, in spite of my stepfather's disappointment I was so happy. Michael and I love each other so. They say the Red Rose is a dreadful criminal, but I'm afraid I can't wish him any ill-will. You've always been so kind to me, Betty, that I had to write and tell you all this. Love from us both. —Joan."

Betty thrust the letter under her pillow. "Marie," she said, "if you'll give me that book, I think we may safely write 'paid' after the name of Jabez Blakeney."

EPISODE 3

"Octavius Rodd." Betty Connolly's gold pencil hovered over the name in the little secret notebook which now lay open upon her dressing-table.

She looked pale and excited. Her great grey eyes were dancing and her lips quivered with pleasure.

It was early one morning. She was still in negligé, and the coloured georgette enhanced her pale, fragile beauty. Marie, eager and enthusiastic as her mistress, lingered in the background.

"The third name," said Betty softly. "The others were difficult, Marie, but this time we're really up against something."

Marie nodded. "In some ways Mr. Rodd was the cleverest of them all," she said. "Do you remember—"

Betty closed her eyes. "I shall never forget it," she said simply. "Whenever I think of that ring of scoundrels, those eight men who ruined my home, I see red, Marie. There's no pity, no compunction left in me. I've sworn to make each one of them pay, and I will do it."

The old unfathomable expression appeared in her eyes for an instant. Then she turned to the other girl. "You sent off the warning?"

"Yes," said Marie slowly. "I had it sent off from Hammersmith last night. The police won't learn much from the postmark."

She broke off abruptly, and Betty thrust the notebook hastily into the secret drawer, for there was a soft tapping at the boudoir door.

Marie went out to answer the summons, and came back a little breathless.

"Mr. Kempis is downstairs, Miss Betty," she said. "James says he looks very worried, and wants to know if you can see him right away."

Betty nodded. "Certainly," she said. "Show him up here." She drew the negligé closely about her and glanced at the mirror instinctively to see if her dark hair was in order. Tommy Kempis was a very special visitor.

He came striding in five minutes later in irreproachable morning dress, his brown, handsome face lined and troubled. Marie withdrew discreetly, and the young man took the hand which Betty held out to him.

"You're getting aged-looking, Tommy," Betty said lightly. "I didn't know that being a policeman had that effect upon one."

At her last words a frown spread over Tommy's face, and he sank down into the little blue-brocaded armchair in between the girl and the window.

"It's all very well for you to laugh about Scotland Yard," he said. "I can tell you, they're getting thoroughly hot and bothered. It's this confounded Red Rose again. A man called Octavius Rodd has had a warning sent him this morning. It's just like the others, a single red rose and a card with the word, 'Wellside' printed upon it. The post-

THE DARINGS OF THE RED ROSE

mark is Hammersmith, and the police are searching that district, but I don't see how they can find the Red Rose when they don't know if it's man, woman, or ghost that they're searching for. I say"—he broke off suddenly—"am I boring you frightfully?"

Betty bent forward, apparently to examine the dainty slippers she was wearing, but in reality to hide a smile which she could not repress.

"Not at all," she said. "What's the Red Rose going to do to this Mr. Rodd?"

"That's just the point," the Honourable Tommy Kempis remarked savagely. "That's what's making the Yard so jumpy. No one can possibly imagine what the mysterious crook can be after this time. Rodd is a wealthy man—the Leatherdale Engineering Works must bring him close on a hundred thousand a year—but he doesn't possess any valuables that a thief could possibly steal, nor has he any social aspirations that a disclosure of his fishy past could injure."

Betty laughed lightly. No one looking at her then would have dreamed that she was the famous crook of whom the young man spoke so gravely.

"I don't see why they're so worried then," she said, with a charming assumption of ingenuousness. "If this Mr.—whatever-you-call-him—can't be hurt, why worry about him?"

"Oh, well, you see"—Kempis spoke easily—"the Red Rose has been so curiously successful so far that the police are getting nervy. Rodd himself is a very cool customer. He was most contemptuous about it. I saw him this morning. He said he didn't care for man or devil, and, by heaven, I believe him.

"I never saw such a brute of a man—hard as nails, oozing with money, and as mean as sin. I should rather think he had a lot to answer for, if the truth were known, but you may be pretty sure he's been well inside the law all the time. Of course, he's an immensely important person just now," he went on, talking to himself more than to the girl.

"Look here, Betty can you keep a secret? I think you could help me puzzle out this thing somehow. This man has just landed a Government contract, an affair so secret and important that very few people know anything about it. It will mean everything to his firm if he pulls off the job satisfactorily. Roughly, it's an order to make the more important parts of a new gun. The Government don't want any foreign powers to know that they're even making such a weapon. Now, I can't help feeling that this Red Rose warning is something to do with that."

Betty was not looking at him. She was standing quite straight with her head turned away so that he should not see the startled expression in her eyes. She had thought that that piece of information was a secret from him. The affair was going to be more difficult than she had dreamed.

Betty pulled herself together with a great effort and turned a smiling face on him. "It's all too difficult and complicated for me," she said. "When do you expect the Red Rose to attack?"

"Not immediately," said Tommy. "That is the great thing; it gives us time. The Government haven't parted with the contract yet, and I rather fancy our friend Rodd will bring it back with him after his appointment at the

THE DARINGS OF THE RED ROSE

War Office this afternoon, but, officially, he doesn't expect to have it to show his Board before next Tuesday. There'll be a cordon of police all round the offices from that moment onward. What are you thinking of, Betty?"

She started, reddened, and smiled. "I was wondering if I dared bother you to take me out dancing this evening, as you're so busy, Tommy," she said.

He beamed at her. "Do you really mean it?" he said. "Of course, I'm never too busy for that. I'll come round and fetch you, shall I? What time?"

Betty hesitated. "I'm dining out," she said. "I'll meet you at Ciro's at nine o'clock. How will that do?"

"Splendidly," he said. "I'll leave you now, then." He picked up his hat and cane. "Betty, you're the most wonderful—"

She put up her hand. "Off you go," she said. "Not another word, or I won't come this evening."

He sighed and went off, leaving her staring into her mirror, a half-scared expression upon her face. The moment Marie returned, Betty turned to her. "Things are rather serious," she said. "We shall have to act sooner than I thought."

In the Lift

"Hullo! Hullo! Is that you, Miss Betty?"

Marie's voice on the 'phone was nervous and excited.

"He's just this minute left the War Office. I'm 'phoning from a box in Whitehall. If you go now you'll just make it."

Betty sprang to her feet. She had sat in her private room at the Hotel Superbe waiting for that call for three hours. It was now nearly half-past eight. Mr. Rodd's interview had taken longer than anybody had anticipated, but now, although the vigil had been a tedious one, Betty's heart leapt. It was now a million to one that Mr. Rodd would have the contract on him when he reached his home.

She was clad in the most delicate of lemon-coloured evening gowns, the flounced skirt billowing about her slender ankles and her neck and shoulders completely hidden by a great silver fox wrap, the long fur of which concealed practically all her face.

She walked out of the hotel, and, turning down a side lane, walked through into Lower Regent Street.

It was raining slightly, and so, when she stepped into the shadow of a huge doorway belonging to one of the great blocks of offices which abound in that thoroughfare, there was nothing at all extraordinary in the sight of her standing there. The theatre crowds were passing to and fro, and she looked like any ordinary lady waiting out of the rain for her car to arrive from its parking-place.

However, the moment she was sure she was unobserved she stepped back and instantly was swallowed in the darkness of the doorway. What happened next was accomplished in a little under ten seconds. From her dainty handbag she produced a long thin skeleton key. The great door swung open, a slender, graceful form passed within, then the door closed again, and all was silent.

Like a good many of her sex, Betty had an uncanny gift of finding her way in the dark. She moved noiselessly, creeping down the wide corridor to where the great

THE DARINGS OF THE RED ROSE

ornamental lift stood in an alcove. Then she produced a tiny electric torch, and examined the mechanism. A little sigh of relief escaped her as she recognised the pattern.

It was an automatic affair, controlled by a dial upon the wall of the corridor, the passenger setting the hand to the floor at which he wished to alight, and then closing the gates of the lift to set it in motion. Moreover, and this last discovery sent a thrill of satisfaction to the girl's heart, there was inside the lift a speaking tube which connected with the attendant's office, a tiny compartment in the vestibule, so that an outgoing passenger could order his car as he descended.

Hidden behind a huge pillar, Betty waited. She knew that Octavius Rodd's flat was on the top of the block of offices which he owned. The miser financier lived very simply, and Betty guessed that perhaps save for a single aged servant she was alone in the great building. Since he lived there himself Rodd dispensed with the services of a night watchman.

Five minutes passed, and it seemed to Betty that she had waited so many hours. Then, from somewhere in the darkness, she heard the rattle of a key in a lock. The next moment the door swung open, and the lights were turned up as Octavius Rodd strode down the passage.

He was an immense man, tall and heavy, with close-cut fair hair and a wrinkled, fleshy forehead. His small eyes were set back in his head, and there were pouches of fat beneath them. His mouth was wide and cruel, and his teeth square and uneven. He looked a very formidable enemy.

He walked over to the dial, set the hand to number six, and, switching off the lights, stepped into the lift, which rose up into the darkness as he clanged the gates to.

At the same instant Betty darted from her hiding-place. She reached the dial and swung the hand back until it rested between the numbers four and five. Then, quick as lightning, she ran back to the attendant's office, and put her lips to the mouthpiece of the speaking tube.

Meanwhile, in the tiny, brilliantly-lit lift, suspended helplessly between the two floors, Mr. Octavius Rodd began to swear angrily to himself. His first thought was that the lift had broken down, and it had just dawned upon him that he was in a slightly precarious position, when, clearly and distinctly, from somewhere just behind his ear, a voice said quietly, "Good evening, Mr. Rodd."

It was a high, thin, far-away voice, strangely weird and terrifying in that great empty building.

The financier emitted a sharp exclamation of fear and spun round. As soon as he ascertained that the strange voice was coming from the speaking tube, and not from any supernatural agency he became his old blustering self again.

"What the devil do you think you're doing?" he demanded savagely. "If you don't put me down on the next floor within five seconds I'll—I'll—" His voice ended in a snort, and he began to swear with such vigour and technique that any ordinary listener could not fail to have been impressed.

When he paused, breathless, the same airy voice said gently, "I'm going to drop the lift so that two inches of it overlap the third floor. Through that tiny space you will push the Government Contract—yes, I know you've got it

THE DARINGS OF THE RED ROSE

on you," the voice went on, "and unless you give it up you're not coming out of that lift alive."

There was something so sinister about the last announcement that all inclination to swear suddenly left Octavius Rodd

"Who—who are you?" he demanded unsteadily.

A low musical laugh answered him.

"Do you remember Wellside?" the voice went on pitilessly. "The homes you ruined, the men you drove to suicide?"

"Who are you?" the man repeated.

"Look above your head and you'll see," the voice answered astoundingly. The financier glanced above his head nervously. There, tucked in a crevice of the ornamental roof, was a single red rosebud. A cry escaped him, and immediately afterwards there resounded once again from the speaking tube the same sinister laughter.

Octavius Rodd was frightened, but he was by no means beaten. His was a stubborn, forceful nature, unused to giving way to the demands of others.

"I'm hanged if I'll do it," he said bitterly. "I'll stay here all night rather than do it."

"I'm afraid I can hardly agree to that," the voice assured him mockingly. "Unless you pass out that contract within five minutes, when your employees arrive to-morrow morning they will discover that there has been an unfortunate lift accident. You are now four and a half floors up. If the lift should suddenly be dashed to the ground, I shudder to think what would happen to it, and to you in it. You will hand out that contract, Mr. Rodd."

The man was frightened, but he still fought savagely.

"It's not possible," he shouted.

"The power switch for the whole building is here at my side," the voice answered him. "I have only to pull it up and all the current will be cut off. The lift will drop like a stone. You ought not to have been so economical with your electric installation, Mr. Rodd."

The financier made no answer, and suddenly the lift seemed to drop beneath his feet. He fell upon the floor, cringing, terrified.

For twenty bewildering seconds he was precipitated up and down between the floors. Each moment he fancied must be his last. At length the lift came to a standstill once again, and the same mocking voice said gently, "Hand out that contract, Mr. Rodd."

Every ounce of resistance had left the man. He was bruised and terrified. Feverishly he thrust a package of papers into the darkness. He heard a soft thud as they fell to the corridor floor some six feet below.

Almost immediately the voice, very near this time, and horrible in its very gentleness whispered, "Only the contract, Mr. Rodd, only the contract."

"But I shall be ruined!" the man wailed. All the same, he thrust out a second envelope, and this time the voice answered him approvingly.

"That's better. Much better. Goodnight, Mr. Rodd."

"Aren't you going to let me out?" The man's voice rose to a scream, but there was no reply. Somewhere far off he heard a door close softly. Then all was silent as the grave.

Ten minutes later, whilst the financier was still raging like a caged lion, helpless in his own lift, Tommy Kempis led Betty out on the dance floor at Ciro's. She was cool and radiant, her eyes sparkling, her lips parted in a smile.

"Five whole minutes late," she said. "I've been ages getting here. But I couldn't help it. I had to give someone a lift."

Paid in Full

"It's wonderful, Miss Betty, simply wonderful, but I don't see how we're going to make it benefit Wellside."

Marie stood beside her young mistress, looking down at the official bundle of blue papers lying on the dressing-table. "After all, now we've got the contract, it's as you said, not negotiable. We can't sell it."

Betty turned to her friend and assistant. There was laughter in her eyes, and her lips quivered into a smile. It was late at night, Marie had waited up for Betty to come back from dancing. The younger girl still wore her gown of primrose net.

"We can't sell it," Marie repeated.

"Why not?" said Betty coolly.

Marie shrugged her shoulders. "Who to? There's only one person who wants them, and that's Mr. Rodd."

"Well," said Marie, "why not?"

Marie stared at her. "You don't mean to sell them back to him?" she said. "Oh, Miss Betty, would you dare?"

An excited chuckle escaped the younger girl. "Look here, Marie," she said, "I bet you anything that Octavius Rodd won't admit that this affair has taken place at all—not at present at any rate. Of course, he can't proceed without the contract, because he's got to show it at his Board meeting next Tuesday. But he'll try to get it back before then without anyone knowing. I rather fancy he won't go to the police, and that's where we come in. Listen, get out the typewriter. Now the cheap paper that has no watermark. I think I know just the sort of letter."

Marie produced the tiny portable typewriter, identical with thousands in daily use all over the city, and Betty sat down to her task.

"On the day that the sum of twenty-five thousand pounds is paid to the Secretary of the Wellside Restoration Fund, Wellside, Lancs., the contract inadvertently dropped by you on the evening of the 23rd will be returned intact, and uncopied, by the finder. The money must be paid without condition, a freewill offering in every respect."

Betty took the sheet of paper out of the machine and read it through. "Now we must get this to him somehow," she said. "I rather fancy I've an idea for that, too. This is a job for you, Marie. It must go directly and not be opened by any secretary. That's why the post won't do, this time."

Marie looked up eagerly. "How about the flower girl, Miss Betty?" she said.

The younger girl nodded. "That's just what I was thinking," she agreed.

It was late the following morning when Octavius Rodd stepped out of the front door of his office, anxious and frightened.

Added to the loss of his contract, he had had a sleepless and terrible night, imprisoned in his own lift, helpless until the first arrival released him in the morning.

As Betty had predicted, he had told no one of his loss. The admission involved too many questions.

THE DARINGS OF THE RED ROSE

For two or three hours he had tried to sleep without any success, and now he strode out into the city, uncertain where he was going, or what he was about to do.

He was very irritated, therefore, when he felt a hand upon his wrist the moment he set foot upon the pavement, and heard a cracked voice in his ears whining piteously, "Roses, sir, pretty roses. Buy a rose. Lovely roses. Buy a rose."

He glanced down impatiently, to see an old woman, shabby and indescribably dirty, holding a single crimson bloom towards him, a piece of paper twisted round the stem.

He was about to shake the old creature off savagely, when something curious in her face, something he could not quite understand, made him pause. Then he caught sight of the flower, and every shade of colour fled from his cheeks.

He put out his hand tremblingly and took the rose. The slip of paper attracted him, and he snatched it from its position and shook it out hastily. As he grasped its message a bitter explosion of anger escaped him, and he turned furiously upon the old flower-seller.

He looked about him in vain. There was no sign of the old woman. She had disappeared as if the earth had swallowed her up. As a matter of fact, she had stepped off the curb the moment the financier had taken the flower, and darting through the open door of a waiting coupé, which had then been driven off by its chauffeur, a young and exceedingly beautiful girl with jet black hair and the prettiest laughing eyes in the world.

Meanwhile Octavius Rodd thrust the crumpled note in his pocket. For some hours he wandered about, trying to make up his mind what to do. He realised that he was in a cleft stick. To admit that he had lost the papers would be to lose the confidence of the Government forever.

Without admitting the theft of the papers, he was powerless to call in the police to search for someone who had stolen them. Reluctantly he turned toward his bankers.

It was some mornings later when the Honourable Tommy Kempis again visited the girl, who was such a popular, and yet such a mysterious figure, in London society. He was shown into her boudoir, where he discovered her seated at her little escritoire. She was scribbling in a small notebook, which she put away hurriedly as he entered.

The young man glanced at her admiringly. She looked wonderful in a smart little powder-blue crepe-de-chine frock which enhanced the slenderness of her figure and showed the dark lustre of her hair to perfection.

"Well, my dear sleuth," she said, after their first greeting, when he had sunk down into his accustomed chair, "and how is your precious Red Rose crook this morning?"

He grinned at her, and laughed ruefully.

"You tease me," he said. "As a matter of fact, I was right this time. The Red Rose didn't follow up the warning which was sent to Octavius Rodd. The contract was forthcoming at the Board Meeting yesterday, and all is well."

"Splendid!" said Betty, laughing. "And so the lovely warning was wasted?"

Tommy grinned. "I don't know about that," he said. "Did you see in the paper the other evening about Rodd's gift to the Wellside Fund?"

THE DARINGS OF THE RED ROSE

"I never read the papers," lied Betty.

"Oh, well, it's most interesting." Tommy was amused. "Apparently old Rodd got Wellside on his conscience, for, suddenly, last Friday, the day after the warning, he sent them twenty-five thousand pounds off his own bat, without any palaver. Just went out and did it, like you'd go and buy a new hat.

"And now, my dear, I want to talk about ourselves. I love you, Betty, I—"

The girl laid her hand over his mouth. "Tommy," she said, "you're the most wonderful person that ever lived. But—not now. You mustn't make love to me now. You see, I—I don't really belong to myself yet."

The young man looked so pathetically dejected that her heart yearned towards him. He pulled himself together, however. "Oh, well, we'll talk of other things," he said. "What were you so busy scribbling at when I came in?"

For a moment the girl seemed a little non-plussed. Then her cheeks dimpled into a smile.

"Oh, I was just putting paid to an old account," she said cheerfully.

EPISODE 4
THE LADY AT THE CROSSROADS

"Mr. Lemuel Capet, late of Wellside, Lancs., guarantees to place a donation to the Wellside Fund of twelve thousand pounds in the hands of anyone proving himself to be the Red Rose, in exchange for half an hour's conversation. This offer is straightforward and contains no hidden trap—Advert."

"Did you ever read anything so perfectly idiotic as that announcement?"

Tommy Kempis handed the paper to the beautiful, blue-eyed girl who sat opposite him in the theatre-box. The first interval had just begun, and Betty, radiant in a swathed, maize-coloured gown of mousseline-de-soie, her luxurious evening cloak hanging over the back of the little gilt chairs, its rich sable color enhancing the dazzling whiteness of her skin, smiled at him and leaned forward, and as she did so many people in the stalls and circle, who had recognised her as Lady Derry's beautiful protégée, remarked upon her loveliness to their companions.

She read the advertisement he indicated, and her fine eyebrows rose.

"How very extraordinary," she said, a carefully assumed note of casualness hiding the interest she really felt. "Surely that won't do any good, will it?"

Tommy Kempis sighed and shook his head. He picked up his silver cigarette case from the box rail in front of him and toyed with its contents.

"Of course it won't," he said testily. "That's the irritating part of it. He's simply calling the famous crook's attention towards him. Who's going to answer an advertisement like that? Only a lot of fakes eager to get hold of the money."

Betty frowned. "Who is this Lemuel Capet?" she said, flicking up her long feather to hide her face.

The young man answered her readily. "My dear girl, you must have heard of him. He's one of the wealthiest men in the city. Of course, he was one of the eight financiers who were in that disgraceful Wellside affair which our precious crook seems so interested in. Do you know, Betty, I rather fancy that those eight men have had a consultation."

The girl did not look at him; indeed, she turned deliberately and bowed to an acquaintance she had seen sitting in the stalls, but it was not disinterestedness that made her turn her head. Tommy went on talking.

"Of course, I think they deserve all they get," he said. "It's awfully difficult to put my heart into an attempt to save these bounders a few thousand pounds. But I know they're getting scared, and, anyway, I suppose I must get on with my job and do all I can to help them, which is not easy when they do things like this," he went on bitterly, tapping the paper.

THE DARINGS OF THE RED ROSE

The face that Betty turned towards him was the complete picture of innocence.

"Then you're certain the Red Rose won't answer that advertisement?" she inquired.

Tommy laughed. "The Red Rose will be a fool if he does," he said.

The girl's eyes widened. "Then it's a trap?" she said.

Tommy nodded. "Of course it is. I think we can guess exactly what happened. These eight men had a meeting. Two of them had already been openly victimized, and a third presented a very large sum of money to a Wellside charity in rather a mysterious fashion. Well, I think they were all terrified, and I expect our friend Lemuel Capet put forward his little advertising scheme and they jumped at it as a last hope. It's the silliest thing I've ever heard of, but, of course, what can you expect from a man like Lemuel Capet?"

Betty laughed at the disgust in his face. "Not a nice person?" she said inquiringly.

Tommy grimaced. "Not at all nice," he said with feeling. "A mean, overfed, small-minded person. I may be prejudiced, but he strikes me as not having a single redeeming feature. He has a great estate in the country, where they say his tenants are terrified of him. And not only that," he went on comically, "but he has a great red roll of fat over the back of his collar, and I always hate a man like that."

Betty opened her mouth to speak, but changed her mind and was silent, and at that moment the curtain rose upon the second act of the absorbing play they were witnessing.

But the girl was no longer interested in the story portrayed upon the stage; she sat back in the shadow so that no light from the stage could fall upon her face. As she sat there in the darkness a new expression had crept over that beautiful face. She was no longer laughing, neither had she the strange sad, half-wistful look at which the Honourable Tommy Kempis had so often wondered, but instead there had come into her eyes a new determination, a new daring, which no one had ever seen there before.

The Voice on the Telephone

"Oh, Miss Betty, be careful." Marie spoke earnestly, her strong dark face alight with consternation. "It's not safe."

Betty shook her head. Swathed in a gorgeous tea-gown whose lacquer-red and silver folds clung to her slender figure she stood by her dressing-table, her precious little notebook in her hand. There was new excitement in her eyes and her lips quivered.

"Nonsense, Marie," she said softly. "Don't you see that advertisement gives me an opportunity which I might never get again? Lemuel Capet is a man whose whole life has been devoted to money. Twelve thousand pounds remains a great sum to him in spite of his great wealth. To force him to part with twelve thousand pounds, for the Wellside Fund, of course, will hurt him more deeply than anything else anyone could ever do.

"I have set out to punish these men. I have sworn to do it—to make them pay for the miseries they caused and the sins they committed, and I fancy this advertisement delivers yet another one of them into our hands. Don't be scared,

Marie," she went on, noticing that her staunch friend and associate was now genuinely frightened. "I think I can see our way."

Marie sighed, and a resigned expression crept into her dark eyes.

"All right, Miss Betty," she said, "but there's one thing I beg of you—let me help you. If there's any danger let me share it."

Betty shot a smile at her.

"Thank you, Marie," she said. "I shall need you." Then she moved over to the telephone, and deliberately gave the number which she had just discovered in the 'phone book. Within five minutes she was speaking to Lemuel Capet himself.

The voice on the 'phone was an unpleasant one. It was breathless and inclined to be guttural. Betty's opinion of the man sank even lower than it had been before.

"Hello," she said. "Is that Mr. Capet?"

"Yes," the voice said wonderingly. "My secretary tells me that the Lady Wessex is speaking."

Betty laughed a soft, unmusical chuckle quite different from her own. "I'm afraid you were misinformed, Mr. Capet," she said. "I am ringing up from a call-box in Piccadilly. The is the Red Rose speaking."

There was an audible gasp from the other end of the wire.

"I chose a call-box," Betty lied calmly, still speaking in the strained, soft voice with a threatening note lingering in its depths, "because it occurred to me that you might attempt to trace the call. I don't altogether trust you, Mr.

Capet, but I took the liberty of giving Lady Wessex's name so I might be sure of speaking to yourself."

"How do I know that you are the Red Rose?" the voice came cautiously across the wire.

"Would you like me to prove it to you?" Betty's voice had sunk until it was almost a whisper, and there was something curiously menacing in her gentle, purring tone.

There was silence from the other end of the wire for some considerable time. The Red Rose's exploits were so famous and so dreaded that Lemuel Capet had good cause to be afraid.

"I read your advertisement," Betty went on, "and I thank you. I shall be glad to contribute the twelve thousand pounds you mention in it to those funds which are in most urgent need of them."

Lemuel Capet's voice took on a note of heavy cunning.

"You must come and fetch the money," he said. "I want to see you—that's part of the bargain. When will you come?"

"Aren't you looking forward to interviewing me?" Betty allowed her amusement to sound in her voice. "You will have about forty policemen all round you, I suppose. You must think me a very stupid person, Mr. Capet."

The contempt in her voice stung the man. "Nonsense," he said, "I should be alone."

"That's very brave of you, " Betty replied lightly. "Am I to understand then that you are offering me this vast sum simply because you want to meet me?"

The millionaire answered her slowly. "No," he said, "but I will confess to you that I am afraid. Every man with whom I was associated in a certain incident concerning

THE DARINGS OF THE RED ROSE

Wellside has either received or fears to receive a visit from you. I am anxious to buy myself out, if you understand me. If you will come for the money, you shall have it. I shall not appeal to the police. Do you agree?"

In spite of himself he could not keep the eagerness out of his voice. He fancied that he was bluffing very well.

At her end of the wire Betty smiled to herself. "Splendid," she said.

"Then you'll come?" Lemuel Capet's voice rose jubilantly.

"No," said Betty softly, "we will meet out. I don't fancy your hospitality. Forgive me, but I can't help that. I will send you a note containing full instructions. I should file them if I were you. You will know that the letter is a genuine one by a red rosebud which will be enclosed. Goodbye."

She rang off.

Marie stood quivering beside her mistress. "Oh, Miss Betty, how you dared," she said. "If they should trace the telephone number."

"Well?" Betty shot her a quizzical glance. "Telephone girls sometimes make mistakes, and who would believe their word against mine?"

Marie nodded, but she was still dubious. "I know," she said, "but, oh! it is dangerous. And, besides, what are you going to do now?"

"Wait," said Betty. "I sent a note to Mr. Capet this morning. I should think he would receive it in about an hour's time. It will have an East End postmark. And when we see what effect that has upon him and his friends at Scotland Yard we will decide upon our next movement."

"But what have you arranged?" said Betty miserably. "If we should fail?"

Betty cut her short. "Keep your spirit up, Marie," she said, "and we won't fail. Do you know, Marie, I have an idea that this is going to be the prettiest, neatest affair of all this curious career of ours. And remember," she went on with sudden gravity, "remember what they did to our home."

The Trap

Marie did not have long to wait, as Betty had predicted. The following morning Tommy Kempis called upon Betty. She found him waiting for her when she came in from her morning ride in the park, looking wonderfully fresh and neat in her smart riding habit of black cloth. The young man looked at her admiringly. He was jubilant, and his good humour and excitement were apparent immediately.

"I say, you look wonderful," he said. "Must you dash up to change right away? Can't you stay and listen to my marvellous news? We've got it all taped. This time tomorrow night the Red Rose will be under lock and key."

Betty shot him a single swift glance, and then, seeing that he spoke seriously, she repressed the slow, bitter smile that had risen to her lips. She wondered what his attitude would have been had he guessed the identity of the girl who stood before him.

"You're not interested?" he said, noticing her expressionless face. "How wrong of me to come up here worrying you about things that don't concern you in the least," he went on regretfully.

Betty beamed at him. "Nonsense," she said. "It has a lot to do with me. I read the papers every day most carefully. I'm quite as excited over the whole affair as you or anybody else. Do tell me all about it."

She sat down beside him on the deep leather couch in the old oak furnished morning room.

"How's it going to be managed?" she demanded. "Have you found out who the mysterious person is?"

"Well, not exactly," said Tommy cheerfully, "but we know it's a woman, because she had the audacity to talk to old Capet on the 'phone last night. He came round crazy with excitement this morning. He's had a letter from the Red Rose putting up a most extraordinary scheme to him.

"He is to meet her in broad daylight at eleven o'clock to-morrow morning at Webley Moor, on the Great North Road. There's a famous crossroads there, you know, right in the middle of the moor. Of course, it's quite obvious why she chose the place, because although there's always plenty of traffic on the road, there's no cover for an ambush for at least a mile in any of the four different ways. So she's not a fool—simply an over-daring woman. By Jove, Betty," he went on, his eyes lighting up, "sometimes I can't help admiring her."

Betty dared not look at him lest her eyes should betray her pleasure. Somehow, just lately it had been very difficult for her to carry on with the work she had pledged herself to do, knowing all the time that she was working against Tommy—that Tommy was in reality her enemy. If she could believe that he could ever understand it would make everything so much more easy.

"Apparently," said Tommy, slowly, "old Capet has made her believe that he's acting on the level for once. That's why this scheme of his is rather dirty. Still, I suppose the woman's got to be captured, so there it is."

"What scheme?" said Betty, trying hard to keep any of the anxiety which she felt well out of her voice.

The young man grinned and spread out his elegant shoes to the fire. "Well, it's a bit complicated," he said, "but it works out quite simply. You see, the Red Rose's letter to Capet was like this."

He took a sheet of copying-paper out of his pocket and spread it out for her to see.

"Webley Moor crossroads at eleven o'clock Friday morning," it ran. "Drive up in your car at eleven o'clock sharp. I will meet you there. Hand the money in notes, in a parcel, out of the window. I shall wear a red rose, that is how you will know me."

Betty laughed as she finished reading. "How exciting," she said, "and is Mr. Capet really going to do all this?"

"He's going to obey it the letter," Tommy assured her gravely, "but he's thought out a really neat way of outwitting her. We shall have four police traps on the four roads, each one about a mile from the crossroads, and we shall have a lookout man with a field telephone and glasses on the top of Webley Ben—that's a fairly big hillock also about a mile from the crossroads.

"Old Capet's red Daimler will be perfectly easy to recognize with glasses at that distance. He will arrive at eleven o'clock, and will hand the money to the mysterious

THE DARINGS OF THE RED ROSE

lady. Then he will go back to be well out of danger. Then the lookout man will follow the lady's car with his glasses, see which road she takes, get the description of her car, and simply telephone it to whichever police trap she is bound to pass. There, you see, that's the scheme—rather elaborate, but it can't fail, can it?"

"I shouldn't think so," agreed Betty slowly.

"That's what pleasing old Capet so," said Tommy. "I'm afraid I shall be on the job myself; I may be the lookout man. I don't like the idea. It seems rather mean after the fellow has made her believe that he is going to pay up."

Betty did not answer; the old thoughtful expression had returned to her eyes. Tommy changed the subject.

"When shall I see you again?"

"I don't know," she said lightly. "I'm going up North myself tomorrow morning early to stay for a day or two with Lady Derry."

He glanced at her hopefully.

"That's at Derry Hall, isn't it?" he said. "Perhaps after this thing is all over I could come along?"

Betty smiled at him. "I'm sure you could," she said gracefully.

But the moment he had left the house she sent for Marie, and the other girl saw, as soon as she entered the room, that something unusual was afoot. Betty's eyes were dancing, and there was an expression of reckless daring in their blue depths.

She outlined the details of Mr. Capet's plan as she had heard it from Tommy, and laughed at Marie's involuntary exclamation of apprehension.

"Don't worry, Marie," she said. "I've got a wonderful scheme. I think we can trick Mr. Capet with his own idea. Listen. You know he has a famous red Daimler? Well, it won't be difficult for us to hire another one exactly like it, or, anyway, near enough to confuse anyone who was watching with field-glasses from a distance of a mile or so. And this is where you come in. We shall need three cars to-morrow, Marie. Do you see my plan?"

The other girl hesitated. "I think I can guess," she said. "You're going to make them think it's all over before it's really begun, so that they stop the wrong car."

Betty laughed. "Splendid, Marie," she said. "You're coming on."

At the Crossroads

At five minutes to eleven on the following day a magnificent red Daimler pulled up at the crossroads on Webley Moor. Its colour gleamed in the sun, and it looked curiously self-conscious, as if it knew that far away on the hillock, to the right, Tommy Kempis was watching it, his glasses trained upon it shining body work.

Seated at the wheel was a man dressed as a chauffeur, but his face beneath the peaked cap was the face of Marie's friend and assistant, who had done so much for the Red Rose in one of her earlier exploits.

Betty's attempt to get a car resembling that of the millionaire had been completely successful, and Tommy Kempis, watching through his glasses, was utterly deceived.

Almost immediately afterwards from down the road on the west came a second car, a black saloon of a very dis-

THE DARINGS OF THE RED ROSE

tinctive design. It came to a full stop at the corner, and a woman, heavily veiled and dressed in black, stepped out on to the road.

Tommy Kempis, watching her through his field glasses, felt his heart rise in his mouth as he saw her. He could not recognise Marie at that distance, nor did he see the smile upon her face as she ran across to the red Daimler and took something from the driver's hand. After a hasty word with her accomplice chauffeur she returned to the black car, and, stepping in, was driven off at speed up the North Road towards the waiting police trap.

"Black saloon," he said breathlessly, "old-fashioned type, coming your way. Girl dressed in black from head to foot. Get her; hold her till I come."

He heard the sergeant's cheery "Righto, sir," and then, anxious to be present at the denouement, he scrambled down the hill as fast as he could go, making for his motor cycle, which was waiting for him at the roadside. So engrossed was he that he did not notice a little grey two-seater which had been speeding down the London road and had now come to a stop at the crossroads. Almost immediately afterwards the thing that Betty had hoped for happened.

Sailing down the road toward the two-seater came a second red Daimler, almost identical with the car that had given Tommy such a thrill not five minutes before, and inside it, nervous and excited, sat Lemuel Capet himself. He was not a pleasant sight to look upon, as he folded and unfolded his podgy hands across his capacious waistcoat. The brown paper bundle of notes was at his side, genuine notes all of them, since unless the police could prove that the Red Rose had taken actual money from the millionaire their case against her might be difficult to prove.

Capet was frightened. He realised, perhaps better than any of the other financiers, exactly what their coup of long ago had meant to the Wellsiders, and he could not get away from the feeling that perhaps now the day of reckoning might be at hand.

His chauffeur had been told nothing, save that he was to stop at the crossroads. He did so, drawing up alongside the two-seater.

To the millionaire's surprise an old lady got out of the smaller car, and came mincingly toward him. He thought at first that she was some unfortunate person who had lost her way, and as the bent figure advanced towards him, some of his courage returned. The old woman advanced to the window, beside which the financier was sitting. Her face was almost hidden by a scarf and her voice chilled him immediately. It was the same soft, terrifying voice he had heard across the wire.

"Give it to me, please," she said softly, and at the same time dropped a red rosebud onto his lap.

The effect of her strange appearance flabbergasted the man, and quite simply he handed her the parcel, leaned back in his seat, stirring himself only enough to signal to his chauffeur to turn and go back.

Meanwhile, the strange old lady with the curiously youthful eyes had returned to her car, tossed the brown paper parcel into the back, and then leapt into the driving seat with surprising agility, and the next moment was speeding away up the North Road as if she had not a care in the world.

THE DARINGS OF THE RED ROSE

The police trap, having received no instructions, did not attempt to stop her, and she sailed past them without any trouble. Once out of sight she increased speed, and took to the lonely roads, the little, winding lanes that led her through small towns and half-forgotten villages until any attempt to follow her would have been impossible, and then, at the sanctuary of a little cottage where an old woman, a friend of her Wellside days, awaited her, she pulled up. And fifteen minutes later Betty Connolly, her disguise removed, drove, smiling and chic as ever, on her ways towards Derry Hall.

It was late that evening before Betty and Marie could compare notes. It was only when they were up in the great old oak bedroom in Derry Hall, the leaping firelight making strange shapes on the ceiling and deepening the shadows among the silken drapery of an old four-poster bed, that the two girls were able to talk. Marie's eyes were shining.

"Oh, Miss Betty," she said, "what a wonderful idea. It was a real brainwave thinking of the second red Daimler. You should have seen Mr. Kempis's face when he got to the police trap and found it was me that they had held up. I did everything just as you told me. I explained that when we reached the crossroads I saw my young man, who is a chauffeur, alone in his master's car. He called me over and gave me a box of chocolates for my birthday present.

"I showed the police the chocolates. They searched the car, though, and Roberts, Lady Derry's new chauffeur, was furious, but of course he bore me out in my story because he had seen my boy give me the sweets. He didn't know he wasn't a real chauffeur and that we had hired the car, so, of course, at last they let us go on."

Betty laughed and nodded. "Marie, if you'd seen that horrible man shaking all over like a jelly when he handed me the notes, even though he thought I was a poor old woman, you'd have had hysterics," she said. "We'll get the money off to the Wellside Fund in a day or two, when the excitement has died down. Meanwhile, the police can go on hunting for the lady who drives so well; and good luck to them."

The two girls went on laughing and talking until suddenly Marie glanced at her young mistress shrewdly.

"It's a pity about Mr. Kempis, isn't it, Miss?" she said. "It seems as if he's on the wrong side."

"Oh, I wish, Marie—" she began, and checked herself. "No," she said resolutely. "I won't think of him. I won't think of love until my work is done. And now, Marie, if you'll bring me the book, I want to make a small but satisfactory tick against the name of financier number four."

EPISODE 5
THE GIRL ON THE FIRE-ESCAPE

Betty Connolly, society girl and mystery to her friends, stood in the doorway of the poverty-stricken room and held her breath. Tears of pity stood in her eyes. Kneeling by a cot at the far end of the room was a thin, dishevelled woman, who yet bore the traces of the great beauty that had once been hers. She had been crying, and her pale cheeks were still wet. In the cot lay a child, a poor, fragile little creature, whose tiny body was wasted by lack of proper nourishment and the ravages of disease. The mother turned to the girl in the doorway.

"It was good of you to come, Miss Connolly," she said. "Heaven knows how grateful I am for all your kindness to me. Ever since you first helped me three months ago you have done more than anyone could expect of a friend, though I don't know what I have done to deserve such kindness from you."

Betty came slowly across the room and laid her hand on the woman's shoulder.

"My dear Mrs. Clayton," she said, "you must thank Marie, not me. When she first told me you came from Wellside, my old home, that was enough to make me do anything in my power to help you. How is the kiddie to-day?"

The mother sank down upon the floor and looked up at Betty with helpless eyes.

"It's no good, Miss Connolly," she said. "I took him to the doctor again last night. He tells me there's no hope for him unless he has the most expensive treatment in the world. Oh, no," she said hastily as Betty opened her mouth to speak, "for my child's sake I would ask you if I thought you could help me, but this treatment is so expensive that it would more than ruin you, my dear. It's just out of the question, that's all."

She bowed her head and the tears fell down upon her worn hands. In its cot the child stirred feverishly. Betty knelt down beside the woman. Her voice was very gentle and there was a great sweetness in her lovely face.

"Mrs. Clayton," she said, "you never told me your story. Forgive me if I seem over-inquisitive, but isn't there anyone in the world whose duty it is to help you?"

She hesitated.

"I remember hearing of your husband's name when I was a child in Wellside, and I always fancied that he was comparatively well-to-do."

The woman nodded. "He was," she said, "and he would never have left me and my baby in poverty had he been able to help it, poor man."

She seemed on the verge of confiding in Betty, and the girl, who had often wondered at her silence, bent forward eagerly.

"Tell me," she begged.

THE DARINGS OF THE RED ROSE

The mother looked at her, and the girl was startled by the sudden look of hatred which was visible in her mild eyes.

"Very well," she said suddenly with a new determination in her tone. "You're the first person who has ever heard this story, Miss Connolly. I've been proud—too proud to advertise my wretchedness. My husband was an engineer. We were happy and fairly prosperous, and then my husband perfected an invention which he had given up half his life to work upon."

She looked up and spoke dramatically.

"That invention, Miss Connolly, was the Dulverton Ore Extractor."

"The Dulverton Ore Extractor?" Betty stared at the woman in amazement. "But that is one of the most famous machines in the world. That is the invention which, they say, made Everard Benham a millionaire."

An expression of indescribable loathing appeared on the mother's face.

"Everard Benham," she said, "yes, that is the man."

Betty's interest deepened as the woman went on. "My husband had just completed his invention when I fell ill. He had spent most of his capital on the machine, and for the time being we were hard put to it. Then Everard Benham came into our lives. He was wealthy even then, and my husband, in his despair, took his invention to this man in the hope that he would see its value and advance us sufficient money to keep us going through my illness. My husband was a simple man. He told the whole story. Benham saw his opportunity, and by a series of clever promises and assurances of good faith, actually induced my husband to part with his life's work for the paltry sum of fifty pounds."

She paused, and her eyes met Betty's steadily.

"Do you know, Miss Connolly," she said slowly, "that is the only money we ever received from him for that machine, which has since made him a multi-millionaire."

Betty did not speak, but her beautiful face had taken on that expression which her friends had come to know so well. The woman went on.

"After that our downfall was steady. When my boy was born my husband appealed to Benham for assistance—only to have the door slammed in his face. Only six months ago in my husband's last illness I myself went to him, driven by despair to attempt to fight for what was mine. He laughed at me, Miss Connolly. Never shall I forget the expression on that loathsome face. I came away without a penny, and my husband died, a broken-hearted man, ruined, and, as I see it, murdered by this fiend, who is now living on the products of my husband's brain."

Betty could not trust herself to speak for some moments. Then she rose to her feet and glanced tenderly towards the sleeping child.

"Mrs. Clayton," she said, "you cannot have your husband back, but I think I can promise you at least some redress from Everard Benham. You will need great courage," she went on quickly, "but I can promise you success in the end. Will you help me?"

The woman nodded gravely. "I have nothing more to lose," she said. "If my child dies my life will be over. I am desperate. Anything to save him—anything in the world."

THE DARINGS OF THE RED ROSE

"I'll come back, then," said Betty; "after I have made a few preparations. In the meantime keep up your spirits and rely on me."

Half an hour later she stood before the dressing-table in her own room in Lady Derry's house in Mayfair, not two miles from the slum where she had spent the morning. The secret drawer lay open, and in her hand Betty held the little red notebook which contained eight names, whose owners had good reason to fear the Red Rose. The girl's face was very grave, and her eyes burned with anger. The fifth name in the list in her hand was that of Everard Benham.

The Changeling

The Honourable Tommy Kempis leaned back in his armchair in the drawing-room of Derry House and surveyed the girl opposite him with frank disappointment in his face.

"I had set my heart on taking you out to dinner to-night, Betty," he said. "Can't you possibly postpone your other engagement?"

Betty shook her head. "I'm very sorry, Tommy," she said, "but a very old friend is coming to see me this evening. Won't you take me out to-morrow?"

He rose to his feet and stood looking down at her. "You treat me awful bad, you know," he said wistfully.

The words were spoken lightly, but the girl reddened. "I know I do, Tommy dear," she said, and added before she could stop herself, "worse than you think, I believe."

He looked at her curiously, but made no comment, and she, as though to change the conversation, said easily, "How is Scotland Yard?"

He grimaced. "Frankly, Betty, I'm getting tired of this Red Rose business. I think the authorities are, too. What seems to happen is that some unpleasant person announces that he has had a warning from the Red Rose, and then, for some apparently inexplicable reason pays over an immense sum to the Wellside Fund, and we hear no more about the matter. Really, I think the next person who complains about the Red Rose had better not rely too much upon police protection. I'm afraid," he added ruefully, "that my sympathies so far have always been with the crook. The victims have invariably been such unpleasant people."

A quick, happy smile spread over the girl's face, but she controlled the little cry of pleasure which had risen to her lips.

"You're a dear, Tommy," she said gently, "but you must go now. You don't mind, do you?"

He went unwillingly. "I shall come again to-morrow," he said, then, smiling at her quickly, he went out of the room.

He was very disappointed. The fragrance of the perfume she wore still lingered in his nostrils, and he could not get the vision of her beautiful face and grave eyes out of his mind.

Meanwhile, in spite of her real affection for Tommy, Betty did not wait long thinking about him just then. She watched him disappear down the street from the window, and, having satisfied herself that he was safely away, she

THE DARINGS OF THE RED ROSE

turned and ran up to her own room, where Marie, white-faced and anxious, was waiting for her.

"It's twenty minutes to seven, Miss Betty," she said. "The Benhams dine at seven, as we found out this morning. You've only got half an hour to do the whole thing."

Betty nodded grimly, and began to scramble out of her afternoon gown and into a plain, black satin robe that lay waiting for her.

"Is Mrs. Clayton here with the child?" she said.

Marie nodded. "She's awfully brave," she said. "Of course, she knows it's for the best, but a mother's got to have courage to part with her child even for so short a time."

Betty nodded. "I know," she said, "she's a wonderful woman. You must remember though, Marie, she's at the end of her tether."

As she spoke she was fitting a tight black cloche hat over her dark curls.

"And the car?" she said suddenly.

"Waiting," said Marie promptly. "My boy's at the wheel, as you arranged. Oh, Miss Betty, I wish you all the luck in the world."

Betty took a black veil from a drawer and wound it round her face.

"Marie," she said softly, "go and get the baby, put him in the car, and then stay with Mrs. Clayton until I come back. I have something to write first, so hurry."

Five minutes later the slim, black-clad figure sped silently down the back staircase and out of a side door to where a dark limousine awaited her. As she came forward

Marie stepped out of the car and laid her finger against her lips.

"He's asleep," she said. "Poor mite."

Betty nodded to her. "You've told the driver where to stop?" she murmured, and, receiving the girl's assurance, slipped into the car and sank down among the cushions. At her side lay little Bobby Clayton, a wasted little figure three years old. The child was wrapped in a long black shawl which completely hid his white clothes.

All through the short drive through the wide Mayfair streets Betty's heart was thumping wildly against her side, but never for one moment did she swerve from the purpose she had set herself. The journey came to an end at last. Betty stepped out on to a narrow, deserted path flanking the grounds of a great mansion. Even as she did so somewhere in the distance a clock struck seven. She steeled herself for the effort. She had not a moment to lose. With a murmured word to the driver to wait for her, she lifted up the sleeping bundle in the car and, holding him close to her heart, she crept into the shadow of the shrubbery.

To get into the grounds was comparatively simple. Her two faithful helpers had prepared a plan of the house and grounds, but as she crossed the broad lawn and came up towards the great building, the next part of her journey looked difficult.

A great fire-escape zig-zagged its way up the side of the house, and it was to this that she crept, keeping well in the shadow. She climbed, silent as a ghost, to the first storey, then to the second, and outside a certain window, heavily curtained, and shrouded from the night, she paused, holding her breath.

THE DARINGS OF THE RED ROSE

She had chosen her time well.

Downstairs in the great dining-hall, Everard Benham was entertaining a tableful of friends. He was clothed with as much elegance as money could buy him. His little piggy eyes glittered and his heavy cheeks were flushed with wine and with satisfaction.

He was completely happy, little dreaming that above his head there hovered a vengeance that would strike at the most precious thing he possessed. Nor did he dream that his host of ill-paid servants were downstairs in their own quarters, not one of them guarding the baby which lay sleeping in the elaborate nursery two floors above his head.

Little Lawrence Benham, the baby heir, lay asleep in his nursery. He was a heavy child, completely spoiled by too much indulgence, and he slept soundly. There was a night-lamp by his bed, which shed a faint radiance over the elaborately-furnished room.

Suddenly the great curtains over the window at the far end of the nursery stirred slightly. A slender figure entered, something held tightly in her arms. So quietly did Betty move that the regular breathing of the two children did not waver. She paused for a moment looking down at the wealthy child sleeping so healthily in its silk-hung cot, and then at the little white face pressed to her breast. A sob rose in her throat.

Very gently she set her burden down on a nearby couch, and advanced noiselessly towards the other child. The substitution was the work of a few moments. Three minutes later she again crept towards the window. This time a lighter bundle lay in her arms, while, still sleeping soundly, little Bobby Clayton lay in the silken sheets of the cot, a note and a red rosebud lying upon the coverlet.

The descent down the fire-escape was perilous. As her foot touched the ground she fancied she heard a sound behind her, and paused, every nerve tingling. But it was only a laugh from the great dining-room, beneath whose window she stood, a fat laugh full of self-satisfaction and conceit.

Betty moved silently on to safety.

A Man at Bay

"You have disregarded my warning, but that in itself is nothing to your heinous crime of the past. This is the child of Robert Clayton, the man you robbed, the man whose brains have made you wealthy. This child is ill. Nothing but the finest treatment in the world can save him. As you treat this child, so will your own be treated. This is not a threat; it is a plain statement of fact."

A red rose was pinned to the letter.

Everard Benham pored over the letter, which lay upon his desk. He sat looking at it all night. He knew he was beaten, and great dark lines had appeared through the flabby flesh of his cheeks. He had not given the alarm yet, although it was a good six hours since the discovery of the substitution of the one child for the other had been made.

The reason for this was obvious. The story would go straight to the newspapers, and the discovery of the manner in which he had swindled the inventor of the machine which had made his fortune would provoke such criticism as might ruin his business projects. He was helpless as he sat there pondering.

Already he had sent for a doctor for the inventor's child. Frightened nurses were moving about over his head. The child was in good hands. Gradually the hours went by, and dawn found him still sitting there. He remembered bitterly how he had ignored the Red Rose's first warning. He remembered how he had tossed the paper and flower into the open grate, and had not even troubled to report the matter to the police.

He was still there staring dazedly in front of him when a bewildered secretary brought in the morning's letters. He turned them over idly, hardly realising what he was doing. Then suddenly something about one of them attracted him. It was heavy, and there was a curiously sweet odour attached to it. With trembling hands he ripped open the flap, and a cry escaped him as a single red rosebud fell out upon the wooden desk. There was a single sheet of typewritten paper within. The message was curt and to the point.

"Your child is safe," it ran, "but only so long as Robert Clayton's child receives careful attention. There is one way out for you.

"The moment that we hear from a reputable lawyer that the sum of twenty-five thousand pounds is being placed at an account made out in Mrs. Clayton's name, and that her child is safe at one of the best nursing homes in the city, all expenses for three months paid in advance, your own child will be restored to you. This is letting you off very lightly considering the enormous fortune you have amassed from the Dulverton Ore Extractor. Any attempts to frustrate this arrangement will be attended by neglect of your child."

Alone in his room the financier stormed, but from the very beginning he was a beaten man. With the aid of the police he knew he might yet frustrate the Red Rose, but with the entry of the police would come the entry of the newspapers. The whole story would come out, and at any rate his social ruin would be complete.

For an hour he cogitated, twisting this way and that, but finally he was compelled to send for his lawyer, and the two of them set out for the bank.

Tommy's Clue

Two days later little Lawrence Benham was found in his father's garden very little the worse for his adventure.

Everard Benham did not make any attempt to revenge himself. He had learnt his lesson, and realised too well the strength of the enemy he would have to combat. The Red Rose's letter, which he had obeyed scrupulously in his helplessness, had made its impression upon him, and he did not attempt to seek out the mother of the child, who was receiving treatment at the most expensive nursing home in London.

Meanwhile, not very far away, in her own boudoir at Lady Derry's house, Betty interviewed a very different woman from the grief-stricken mother who had poured out her sorrows not a week before. Mrs. Clayton was a happy woman. Her eyes were shining, and some of the old beauty had returned to her tired face.

THE DARINGS OF THE RED ROSE

"Miss Connolly," she said, "I can't tell you how happy I am. It seems as if a fairy story had come true. I'm going off to see my boy now. He's looking better already, and they tell me at the nursing home that they are confident that they can not only save him, but make him as strong and healthy as any other boy. I shall have enough now, too," she went on brightly, "to educate him properly. Oh, if only I could do something for you in return."

Betty looked at her gravely. "There is only one thing, Mrs. Clayton," she said, "and that I must beg of you. Never, never, as long as you live, breathe a word of this business to anyone. Keep this secret forever. No one must ever know that Betty Connolly had anything to do with you in this business. You will promise me, won't you?"

Mrs. Clayton nodded, and there was complete sincerity in her eyes.

"I think I can understand," she said. "You can trust me, Miss Connolly. No one shall ever know anything from me."

She went off joyfully, a new spring to her step, a new hope in her eyes. Marie let her out by the side door, and as she hurried back to the boudoir encountered Tommy Kempis in the hall. She smiled at him. Marie had a very soft spot in her heart for the young man of whom her mistress was so fond.

"I'll take you up at once," she said in response to his eager question. "Will you come this way, sir?"

Betty looked up as the young man was announced, and rose to meet him.

"How good of you to come to see me," she said. "Sit down and have a cigarette, and tell me all about yourself. You look worried."

"I am," he said, and added laughingly, "at least not worried, only vaguely curious about something. You know that perfume you were wearing the other night, Betty? Is it very exclusive?"

The girl hesitated. Like many other society women, she followed the fashion of having a perfume specially distilled for her. It was her own exclusively, no one else being sold exactly the same mixture.

The young man leant back in his chair. "If I tell you why I ask you'll think I'm crazy," he said. "However, I'll explain. The other night a frightened nursemaid came to the Yard with an extraordinary story about a child being kidnapped from one of the great Mayfair houses. As she came without the permission of her employer, and as we received no other information, the Yard did not take up the matter officially. However," he went on, "as she told us that a red rose was discovered in the cot where the child had lain I followed the scent myself.

"The girl smuggled me into the house and I looked round. I won't bother you with the details of the story, which were so fantastic I don't think the girl could possibly have invented them, but of one thing I'm perfectly certain—someone entered that nursery, climbing up the fire-escape, and took a sleeping child from its cot. Whether any human being would have the courage I don't know, but although I looked round carefully, there was only one clue that I could discover, and that was this. The room smelt

THE DARINGS OF THE RED ROSE

faintly but quite distinctly of the same sort of perfume as you were wearing the other night, Betty."

Just for an instant the girl seemed to lose her nerve beneath his calm, steady gaze, in which there was as yet no hint of suspicion. The next instant, however, she was herself again.

"I'll ask my perfumer for a list of his clients if you like, Tommy," she said with a forced lightness. "How will that do?"

"Splendid," he said enthusiastically. "You're a wonderful girl, Betty. I sometimes wonder," he went on gravely, "if you realise just how marvellous you are."

"Oh, Tommy," she broke out involuntarily, "I wonder—" She checked herself just in time, and although he begged her to explain she would not tell him the question that was becoming an increasing problem to her.

If he was told the truth, if the whole facts of the case were presented fairly to him, would his love stand the test, would he understand?

EPISODE 6
THE WATCHER BEHIND THE CURTAIN

Betty Connolly stood near the window of her little blue and silver room, her eyes fixed thoughtfully upon the paragraph in the gossip pages of the paper in her hand. On the side table before her lay the famous little red notebook, open.

Slowly, Betty turned, and beckoned to Marie, her faithful little maid and companion, who hovered in the background.

"Listen," she said, and began to read—"'Additional interest will be lent to Mrs. Guggenheim's society concert at the Intimate Theatre, Cranbridge Square, on Thursday afternoon, by the fact that the jewels in the Faust scene in the second part will be none other than the famous Carstairs Rubies, lent for the occasion by the well-known financier, Gustav Wild. These rubies are said to be the finest in the world, and were acquired by Mr. Wild from the executors of the late Maharajah of Limbatala. Miss Dora Fernley will play the part of Marguerite, who discovers the jewels in her casket.'"

Betty put down the paper and glanced at her friend. "Well?" she said.

Marie stared at her. "Why, Miss Betty," she said, "surely you don't suggest that you are thinking of"—she hesitated—"well, of getting the Carstairs Rubies? Why, it's impossible."

The old half-wistful, half-bitter smile passed over Betty's beautiful face.

"Marie," she said slowly, "the name of Gustav Wild is the next on my list. He has retired from business, and unless I rob his private safe at the bank it seems impossible for me to get even with him. Then comes this heaven-sent opportunity. Do you realise what enabled Mr. Wild to buy these rubies upon which he had set his heart?"

A flicker of understanding passed over Marie's face. "Oh, Miss Betty," she said, "was it—was it—"

Betty nodded. "Wellside. It was the wreck of our home, Marie, the degradation and ruin of our own people, that enabled him to buy these jewels. It isn't as if he bought them for a wife, or daughter," she went on passionately, "although that would have been bad enough. He bought them for himself.

"In the ordinary way they are kept at his bank. The task of getting hold of them would have been a well-nigh impossible one, but now, just when I was in despair, along comes this society show. I suppose Wild is attempting to buy himself a place among the best people by this loan of the jewels. Well, we shall see."

Marie's eyes grew round with horror. "I know," she said passionately, "but since there is no justice to punish this man for what he did to Wellside, then I must risk that justice that would punish me for robbing him of what he has no right to own. You will see, Marie. The Wellside fund will receive his donation in spite of himself."

Marie shivered. "Take care," she whispered, "and at any rate let me help."

"I shall need you," Betty promised. "This afternoon," she went on quickly, "I shall go to a dress rehearsal of the show to discover just how the problem is to be attacked. It's not going to be easy—I recognise that. But at the same time I shall do it, if it's the last thing I do."

The dress rehearsal of the society concert is very often quite as much of a society function as the actual performance itself, and Mrs. Guggenheim's was no exception to the rule. As a protégée of Lady Derry's, Betty had no difficulty in obtaining an invitation to the rehearsal. She came into the auditorium of the pretty little green and gilt theatre somewhat late in the afternoon and sat down unobtrusively in one of the side stalls. The "Faust" number had just begun, and Betty watched the stage with great interest.

With characteristic sang-froid the producers of the performance had altered the opera a little to make what they considered was an attractive scena. Marguerite was shown poring over the golden casket supposed to have been sent her by Mephistopheles, and taking out the jewels one by one. As it was just a rehearsal Betty noticed that the jewels were represented by a string or so of beads, whereas the Carstairs rubies would be used on the actual afternoon.

After her song Marguerite was shown to have resisted the temptation, and the curtain came down with her walking slowly off the stage. It rose almost immediately, however, to show her returning, a stealthy figure shrouded in white, taking the jewels from their box, and creeping out with them. Then once again the curtain descended.

Betty caught her breath. The plan she contemplated was so daring it almost frightened her. Yet her brain was ice-cool. She observed Miss Dora Fernley, the girl who played Marguerite, with cold calculation. She was just about her own height and figure, and her hair was dark. There the likenesses ended. Betty drew a deep breath. The plan was a desperate one, but she was determined to go through with it. She was just about to rise and slip quietly out of the building when someone dropped into the seat beside her. It was Tommy Kempis.

"I thought it was you," he said, bending forward. "I caught a glimpse of you in the light from the stage. I had to come over. I didn't know you were interested in this sort of thing."

Betty forced herself to smile. She was not at all anxious to see anyone just then and Tommy least of all. Now that the situation had arisen, however, she made the best of it.

"Of course I'm interested," she said, "but I had to come along to the rehearsal because I can't come to the show tomorrow. It's very good, don't you think?"

He looked at her shrewdly, a little smile playing round his mouth.

"No need to be polite to me," he said. "It's just as bad as these shows always are. A wicked waste of time, I call it. I shouldn't be here at all if it wasn't for my cousins. Mother insisted that I was to appear interested, and I couldn't hurt the old dear's feelings. My cousins play the 'Three Graces' earlier on, you know. Are you here alone? Can't I drive you home?"

THE DARINGS OF THE RED ROSE

The last thing Betty wanted just then was light conversation, and she was a little afraid of Tommy. Afraid because she was so fond of him, and the thought of his horror had he known the project in her mind almost made her shrink from the task she had set herself. She pulled herself together, however, and when she walked out through the foyer to Tommy's waiting car she was chatting with as much animation and lightheartedness as if Mr. Wild and his famous rubies had never existed.

But beneath her smiling exterior her heart was beating wildly, and for the first time in her life there was something akin to fear in the depths of her eyes.

The Shadow in the Limelight

"I've had my orders, Miss Betty. You can rely on me and on my boy."

Marie, smart and neat in a close-fitting black costume and little helmet hat, attempted to smile reassuringly as she spoke, but she could not keep the fear out of her eyes.

Betty was very pale also. She was clothed in white from head to foot. It was an evening gown of the latest fashion, with a long tight corsage which flowed down into long graceful draperies, swinging loosely from knee to ankle. Round her shoulders was a long black velvet cape lined with white silk. When she wrapped the cloak tightly about her she was almost completely hidden, so ample were its folds. Betty held out her hand.

"This may be the last throw, Marie," she said. "If—if anything should happen you must keep your promise. Let me take all the blame. Now, are you certain what you have to do?"

Marie nodded. "There's a window in the back of Miss Fernley's dressing-room," she said. "My boy will get through there and overpower the maid the moment Miss Fernley goes on for her song. Then I shall be waiting, and the moment he gives me the all-clear I will climb in and wait for Miss Fernley herself when she comes back for the first time. I'll pretend I've got her other dress waiting for her, and I'll hold her up until I hear the applause the second time."

Betty sighed. "I don't like getting you into this, Marie," she said. "It's dangerous."

Marie smiled valiantly. "Don't you worry about me, Miss Betty," she said, "it's you I'm worrying about. When I think of you walking on there in front of all those people I—"

"Hush!" Betty slid a hand over her mouth. "Don't worry. There's nothing to be scared about. The detectives watching the jewels are expecting to see a woman in a long white gown come on. I'm relying on them not looking too closely. After all," she added lightly, "there's always some risk, you know, Marie."

"Yes," the other girl, admitted, "yes, of course, but—but this is different. If—if anything should happen you'd be disgraced in front of everyone. Even Mr. Kempis will be there, and—"

Betty shuddered. "Hush, Marie, please," she murmured. "I don't want to think of that just now." She seized the other girl's hand. "Think of that man Wild," she said bitterly, "think of Wellside and the homes and families he ruined."

Marie gritted her teeth and her face set in a grim smile. "I shan't forget," she said.

Ten minutes later Betty's faithful chauffeur set her down in one of the narrow streets at the back of the theatre where the society performance was being held. Like many other theatres, although its entrance gave out upon a broad fashionable street, its sides and back were flanked by narrow ill-lit thoroughfares where furtive figures slunk about with noiseless footsteps.

The stage door was unguarded. Mrs. Guggenheim had seen no need for a stage doorkeeper. Betty looked about her before entering. Save for a big car, whose engine was running silently, there was no vehicle in sight. Betty regretted the presence of the car. She had relied upon all the performers' automobiles being lined up in the rank at the other side of the theatre.

At the moment, however, she had no time to worry about possible sources of danger yet to come. Her present plan of action was important enough to take up all her time. Hastily turning her cloak so that it was now white lined with black she stepped boldly through the stage door. A plain-clothes man standing in a doorway on the right of the long narrow passage in which she found herself gave her a cursory glance, but evinced no surprise. Since it was a society performance the whole place was overrun with beautiful ladies in expensive clothes, friends of one or other of the performers, and Betty went on unchallenged. Still, it had been a breath-taking moment, that second when he had glanced at her idly and decided not to speak.

Penetrating further into the theatre Betty discovered that her task was going to be at once more easy and more difficult than she had anticipated. The place was thronged with people, and the narrow space surrounding the stage was as crowded as the audience.

The centre of attraction was a little bald-headed man with pince-nez. Betty recognised him instantly. It was Gustav Wild. He was evidently very pleased with himself, and his expansive white waistcoat positively glistened and his face radiated self-satisfaction of the most obvious kind.

In an instant all Betty's misgivings vanished. She was consumed with a passionate hatred for this man who had ruined so many innocent people just for the sake of obtaining possession of some jewellery which he could not even wear.

Her chief concern at the moment was fear lest someone should recognise her. She crept into a corner, half hidden by an immense wall of scenery. There she crouched, her heart beating wildly in her side, while with the tip of her tongue she moistened and re-moistened her dry lips. From where she stood hidden she had a very good view of the chattering group round the financier, and the more she saw of Gustav Wild the more heartily she disliked him. He was so very sure of himself, so very certain that he was making a hit with the people about him. Having lent his jewels for the performance he felt he owned the whole place, and was not at pains to hide his belief from anyone.

The stage was all set for the "Faust" scene. With eyes starting and breath coming painfully, Betty watched Gustav Wild place a large golden-coloured casket in the hands of the

THE DARINGS OF THE RED ROSE

stage manager, who stepped through the wings with it and placed it on a small table in the centre of the stage.

Then came Dora Fernley, pale and nervous. Her long white gown trailed upon the floor behind her, and her hair was braided. A sudden misgiving seized Betty. They were really not a bit alike, and she felt her heart rise in her mouth when she contemplated the work she had in hand. She crouched there waiting for what seemed to be hours, yet was in reality only a few moments.

At last she saw Miss Fernley step upon the stage. Then the curtain rose and the girl began her song. The crowd in the wings began to thin considerably as most people went back to their seats in the front of the house to watch the turn. It was said afterwards by a not very tactful critic that Miss Fernley had been chosen for her figure rather than her voice, but at any rate no one listened to her song in such an agony of impatience as Betty, crouching in her corner.

At last, however, the notes died away and the amateur actress drew away from the casket which a moment before she had opened displaying its contents to the audience, those precious glittering gems which had cost a little North-country town so very dear.

The curtain remained up as she came off the stage. She passed quite close to where Betty stood, making for her dressing-room door not three yards away. Just for an instant Betty waited. The dressing-room door closed, and her keen ears caught the sound of a faint scuffle within. Then the curtain began to tremble. In one moment Betty knew that she must walk out, and in front of a theatre full of people snatch the jewels from under their very eyes. And then what she had prayed for happened.

The lights began to dim until there was only a ghostly radiance upon the stage. Like one in a trance Betty moved forward. She had steeled herself to her task, and now that the time had come she did not flinch. Even at that moment she did not forget to act. Covering her face with her hands as though deeply ashamed she crept towards the casket.

Her long white fingers closed over the lid and raised it slowly. Forcing herself to take time she lifted the string of blazing red fire, each stone set in its heavy gold casing, and raised them to her lips. Then turning, she flitted silently across the stage. The audience caught a single glimpse of a fleeting white figure pausing, the jewels pressed to her breast. The next moment she was gone, and the curtain descended amid a thunder of applause.

Trapped

Behind the stage Betty's moment of peril had come. There was just the fraction of a moment between the time when she stepped off the stage and the moment when the curtain should have descended and the lights turned on in a blaze, and at that moment all Miss Fernley's friends would swoop down upon her to offer their congratulations. Betty had to use that moment of darkness.

How she managed to move so quickly she never afterwards knew, but by the time the lights went up she had turned her cloak again, revealing herself standing there swathed in black velvet. One hand clutched the folds of the cape, but in the other, hidden under the flowing garment, she held what was perhaps the most precious collection of jewels in the world, the Carstairs Rubies.

THE DARINGS OF THE RED ROSE

There were still a good many people standing about, electricians, stage-hands, and visitors. Betty knew herself to be in deadly peril. At any moment the substitution might be discovered. She turned and walked with as much casualness as possible towards the stage exit.

Even as she reached the beginning of the long stone corridor she heard a woman's voice talking behind her.

"How silly of Dora to refuse to take her call. She's hidden herself away in her dressing-room, I suppose. I must certainly go and scold her."

Betty heroically resisted the desire to run. Any instant now she knew the hue and cry must begin. She had almost reached the doorway to the street where there was the last plain-clothes man to pass when a figure loomed out of the darkness to meet her.

"Why Betty!" said a voice. "I didn't know you were coming."

The girl felt her senses reel, and a wave of horror passed over her. The voice was Tommy's!

She pretended not to hear him at first, but he laid a hand upon her arm.

"What's the matter?" he demanded. "You're not trying to snub me, are you, Betty? Why," he added as he suddenly caught sight of her face, "what's the matter? I've never seen you look so pale. Are you ill, or—" The words died away upon his lips. From somewhere far behind them in the direction of the stage there had come a scream of horror followed by the cry, "Quick! Thieves! Police!" And then a babel of voices raised in panic broke out.

"Hullo," said Tommy, "what's that?"

His eyes met those of the girl, and just for an instant she felt that she had betrayed herself. The noise at the end of the passage had become intense, and she knew that her agitation must show upon her face. She turned towards the door, but he caught her arm.

"Betty," he said, and in her terror she thought his voice sounded accusing. "What—"

And then a most extraordinary thing happened. From somewhere out of the darkness behind them a form suddenly leapt upon the young man, bearing him to the ground, and before Betty realised what had happened a heavy muffler was thrown over her own face, and she felt herself lifted bodily and rushed forward in the direction of the street.

She struggled wildly to free herself, but she was held in a grip of iron. She had no idea what was happening to her nor into whose hands she had fallen. She felt herself being thrust into a car. The choking muffler over her head almost suffocated her, and she felt herself growing weaker and weaker. She heard the car start and then the sound of cries in the distance, and the blowing of police whistles, but these sounds grew fainter and she realised that she was being rushed through the London streets at terrific speed. Someone was holding her fiercely from behind, but the rubies were still clasped in her hand under the folds of her cloak.

The moment her first panic had passed she began to think more clearly. Very stealthily she tucked the jewels into a tiny pocket in the lining of her frock. Then from her cloak she drew out something small and hard, something which she always carried but as yet never had occasion to use, a tiny silver-plated revolver. All these movements were made surreptitiously, her hand moving quietly under her cloak.

At last the car came to a standstill, and for the first time she heard the voice of one of her captors.

"This'll do, George," he said thickly. "Let's get the stuff and hop it."

"Quiet," said another voice, more refined than the first, "you'll never make a good crook, Joe. You get frightened too easily. I tell you I followed this girl from the moment she came off the stage until the time when you leapt upon her companion in the passage. By the way, I thought I dispatched the plain-clothes man very neatly, didn't you? Now I don't think little Miss Fernley will give us much trouble. She must still have the rubies with her."

Even in the terror of the situation Betty almost laughed. She realised what had happened. She had not been the only person anxious to obtain the rubies that night. Two professional thieves had also been on the watch behind the stage, but she had deceived them quite as much as she had taken in the audience. They were under the impression that they had captured Miss Dora Fernley with the jewels before she had had time to take them to her dressing-room. Betty gripped the tiny automatic and waited.

One of the men stripped the muffler from her face. His companion had stepped down into the road where he stood waiting, leaving the task of obtaining the jewels to his companion, who was clearly the leader. Betty saw that they were upon a lonely strip of road just outside Epping Forest.

"Now," said the man in the car as he turned to the girl seated besides him, "hand over that jewellery, my dear, and we'll let you go. I'm afraid you'll have rather a long way to walk, but we can't help that, can we?"

He smiled unpleasantly at her, and Betty felt her blood rise. Suddenly she bent forward, and the pale light of the stars fell upon the gleaming barrel of her revolver.

"Hands up!" she said.

The man in the car stared at her stupefied, but he did not move.

"Get out of the car," said Betty, her voice cold and commanding.

The next moment a bullet spat into the air about a foot above his head. He almost fell out upon the road. Still covering them, Betty slid into the driving seat. Fortunately it was a make of car she knew, and before the two thieves realised what she was doing she had started the car and dashed off down the straight road at lightning speed, leaving them looking after her utterly bewildered.

Betty drove back toward London, abandoning the car in the suburbs. Then she hailed a taxi and drove home. She found Marie back safely, and the rest of the house in commotion as Tommy had spread the story of the kidnapping.

Her own story was simple. She explained that the thieves had taken her under the impression that she was Miss Fernley, and had abandoned her by the roadside when they found their mistake. Only Marie knew the truth.

It was some days later when Tommy Kempis was seated talking to Betty in her boudoir at Lady Derry's house.

"You know," he said slowly, looking at her, "there's one thing the newspapers don't know. When they found the casket, although the jewels were gone it was not empty. Lying in the bottom of it was a single red rosebud, and

THE DARINGS OF THE RED ROSE

besides that I hear that the Wellside Fund has had a mysterious donation of just about what I should say the jewels would raise if they were sold carefully abroad. You know, Betty I shan't rest until I've tracked down that Red Rose. There's something very curious about him—whoever he is. And of one thing I'm perfectly certain—he's no ordinary crook."

Betty did not answer, but her eyes strayed towards the secret drawer in the dainty escritoire which contained the famous little red book in which yet another name had been crossed off the list.

EPISODE 7
THE WHISPER ON THE PHONE

"And you have made up your mind to take this risk to-night, Miss Betty?" There was a strange ring in Marie's voice as she put the question, a note of pent-up excitement, of eagerness that could hardly be borne.

The two girls were alone together in the big, airy bedroom leading off Betty's blue and silver boudoir. Marie was plainly nervous, but Betty Connolly, standing there, a brightly coloured dressing-gown thrown over her pyjamas, betrayed no sign that this day was to mean any more to her than any other bright and sunny spring morning. She did not answer Marie's question immediately, but stood looking out of the window down the broad street to where the green of the park showed dimly in the distance. She looked radiant, her hair brushed back from her white forehead, her blue eyes deep and mysterious.

Suddenly she thrust her hand into her dressing-gown pocket, and drew out the tiny red leather notebook which held the secrets of so many of the now famous exploits of the Red Rose. Opening it, she handed the book to Marie.

"There," she said, "two more names—and the next one is the most difficult of the whole lot."

Marie looked at the name staring up from the page at her in Betty's girlish handwriting.

"Theodore Windover," she read aloud.

Then a little smothered cry escaped her. "It's impossible," she said. "You know the type of man he is. You must admit that this man is too much even for you."

Betty laughed, and there was a note of spontaneous gaiety in the sound.

"Just because Windover prides himself on being a bully there's no reason why he should be more difficult to manage than anyone else, Marie," she said. "All these weeks, every time I've looked at this book my pencil has hovered over this name. Time after time I have been tempted to take him out of his turn, but now at last his time has come. Of the whole group, Marie, of the whole group of villains Theodore Windover stands out as being the man most deserving of punishment, and here you are trying to persuade me to let him alone."

Marie shook her head vigorously. "It wasn't that," she protested. "I'm so afraid for you, Miss Betty. The papers this morning were full of the elaborate precautions he has taken to protect himself against the Red Rose."

"Is that so?" Betty turned on the girl, her eyes dancing with pleasure. "Get me the papers. I'm longing to see them. My warning stirred him, then."

Marie nodded. "Yes, but hardly in the right way," she murmured. "Far from sending the money which you demanded to the Wellside Fund, he has sent a message to his bankers instructing them to honour no cheque or draft made out by him to the Fund or any of its subsidiary

THE DARINGS OF THE RED ROSE

branches. So, you see, it's going to be difficult from the very beginning."

Betty smiled enigmatically. "When I was a child in Wellside," she said, "I remember seeing a big, coarse man striding through the most distressed parts of the town, his dirty fingers ablaze with jewellery, and an expression of positive pleasure on his face as he glanced from the little shoeless children playing in the gutter to the broken windows of the desolate houses in which they lived. That man was Theodore Windover. I have never forgotten his face. And now at last I believe the time is coming when I shall see it with a very different expression upon it to the one it wore that day in Wellside."

Marie sighed. She realised that once her mistress had made up her mind to go through with the project connected with the cause to which she had devoted herself, no power on earth could dissuade her from her purpose.

"I'll go and get the papers," she said.

Half an hour later found Betty still immersed in the news. The papers had made much of the story of the well-known financier's elaborate precautions against the mysterious power which had threatened him. One paper printed in full the warning which had been sent to Windover.

Betty chuckled aloud when she read her own handiwork reproduced in facsimile under the heading "Mysterious Robber States His Purpose. Your Turn Has Come," the warning ran. "Remember Wellside. Send five thousand pounds for the relief and restoration of the village, or your subscription will be forced from you."

Beneath this was a small paragraph which announced, "We are authorised by Mr. Windover to state that he has definitely made up his mind to refuse to consider the thought of any subscription to the now famous Wellside Fund. He is inclined to ridicule the whole situation, and told one of our representatives yesterday that he had nothing to fear, and considered the whole matter as a particularly foolish practical joke. Mr. Windover has made elaborate precautions to insure that his house shall not be burgled. Mr. Windover, who is very wealthy, amassed a considerable fortune by patenting his electric refrigerators for shops, which have now become famous throughout the world."

The paper then continued to detail the astounding precautions which the financier had made to protect himself. Betty read every word, and then glanced up at Marie, a smile upon her face.

"He's doing it thoroughly, isn't he?" she said. "There seem to be police everywhere. Really, he couldn't be more safe in prison."

Marie sighed. "That's what I've felt all along," she said. "That's why, if you'll forgive me for saying so, it makes it so impossible for you to do anything"

Betty shook her head. "That's all you know, Marie," she said.

"Why, Miss Betty, have you got a plan?" Marie stared at her young mistress eagerly. "Oh, I might have known," she said. "I might have guessed you'd thought of something. Oh, Miss Betty, what is it? Can I help?"

The mysterious expression which had so often puzzled her friends appeared for an instant in Betty's blue eyes.

THE DARINGS OF THE RED ROSE

"I shall need you," she said. "And I shall need your boy, too, Marie. I want a man for this particular idea I have in mind. I've thought it all out, and it seems to me to be the only way."

"Well, we can rely on Jack," said Marie quickly, and added, with apparent irrelevance, "I see Mr. Kempis is not on this case, Miss Betty."

The other girl nodded gloomily. "All the same," she said, "his sympathy is bound to be with them. That's where you're lucky, Marie; you and Jack are on the same side."

She stood for a moment after she had spoken with such an expression of regret in her eyes that Marie dared not speak to her. The next instant, however, she was herself again.

"Come Marie," she said, "we're acting for justice, anyhow. That's the way I look at it, and that's all that really matters. I have sworn that Theodore Windover shall pay, and pay he shall."

The Ambush

Theodore Windover was dozing in his armchair before the remnants of a dying fire when the telephone bell rang. All had been very still in the great oak-panelled library until that moment, and the millionaire woke with a start.

It was one of his methods to have the telephone connected to his own private instrument once his secretaries had retired for the evening. He liked to be at the head of his own affairs, and disdained what he called the "slip-shod business methods" of other wealthy men, who left everything to their employees. Much wealth had changed him very little, and as he sat there in the luxuriously upholstered chair he still looked the coarse, overbearing man whom Betty had remembered so well striding about the streets of Wellside.

His head was bald, and his face almost repulsive, with a spiteful expression lurking in his narrow eyes.

He stretched out his hand for the telephone and put the receiver to his ear. As he did so his eye caught sight of the gilt and marble clock upon the mantelpiece. The hour startled him. It was half-past two in the morning. He could not imagine who on earth could be calling him at such a time, and suddenly a wave of apprehension passed over him.

He brought himself to his senses almost immediately, however, with an angry sneer at his own nerviness. But, nevertheless, his hand shook a little as he held the telephone, and the great black diamond in the ring on his finger sparkled and glinted with an almost uncanny radiance. The ring was Windover's chief personal vanity. It was a magnificent stone, worth a fortune, and utterly unsuited to the hand on which it rested. However, no surroundings could diminish its loveliness, and it glowed against his hand like soft liquid fire.

He spoke aggressively into the 'phone. "Hullo, who's there?"

"Hush, Mr. Windover. Very quietly, if you please."

The words were spoken so softly that Windover fancied that they were whispered in his ear. For a moment he was too startled to reply, however, and the voice went on.

"This is Inspector Gregson, of Scotland Yard, Mr. Windover. You recognise my voice, don't you? I'm speaking softly because I don't want to be overheard."

THE DARINGS OF THE RED ROSE

An expression of understanding, almost of delight, spread over the financier's face.

"You got me worried for a moment, Inspector," he said. "I couldn't think who it was ringing me up at this unearthly hour. Anything to report?"

The other voice sank lower until it was a just distinguishable murmur at the other end of the wire.

"Keep your voice down," it repeated. "You may be watched, Mr. Windover. Don't be alarmed. No harm can come to you. You know my men are surrounding your house."

Windover nodded portentously, quite forgetting that the man at the other end of the wire could not see him. Earlier in the evening he had observed with satisfaction the several pairs of police-constables doing duty outside his house.

"Yes," he said, "you have been very good. But what is the news? Have you caught anybody?"

"We fancy so." There was a note of quiet satisfaction in the tone, which would have deceived anyone. "I am now speaking from inside your store in Maypole Street. Someone is in the building. At any moment now we may make the arrest. That is why I rang you. Is it possible for you to come round immediately? You could meet us at the police station, but I think it would be better if you could come to the actual spot, especially as I know you are anxious to be in at the death."

"Yes, of course. Splendid, Inspector, splendid." There was real triumph in Windover's voice. There was nothing he liked better than to be present at any scene of despair or unhappiness. And, besides, he was proud that, of all his colleagues, he had been the one to frustrate their powerful enemy. "'Phone my chauffeur, and I'll be round almost immediately."

"No, don't do that." The whisper was most urgent. "I'm afraid that the Red Rose may have assistants watching your house unknown to my men. If you call your car you will alarm them immediately, and I don't want any reinforcements. Slip out of the back way and get a taxi; there's an all-night rank quite near you, you may remember. Hurry or you may be too late to witness the actual arrest. When you get to the store go round to the goods entrance in Crosley Street. You'll find I've left the door unlocked for you. When you get inside I'll leave a plainclothes man to direct you. How soon do you think you can get here?"

"Ten minutes," said the millionaire eagerly. "You can rely on me. I'll do exactly as you say, Inspector."

"Hurry," said the voice again, "hurry."

Windover hung up the receiver and slipped out of the room. He was eager and excited. He had had a long conversation with Inspector Gregson a day or so before, and he had fancied that he had not made the favourable impression which it now appeared he had done. Then the inspector had seemed cold, almost inclined to treat him as a nuisance, but now all that had changed. Windover smiled to himself. The fellow had probably discovered just exactly who he was, he decided. Probably he was just trying to curry favour with him. He grinned. He liked people who realised just how important he was. He liked people to keep in their places.

"So they're going to arrest the Red Rose, are they?" he said to himself. "And it's about time, too, that that interfering scoundrel was clapped into jail, where he could be no

THE DARINGS OF THE RED ROSE

more inconvenience to law-abiding citizens." Windover used the word law-abiding with a certain amount of delight. No one understood better than he the amount of shady dealing that could be carried on under that term. He had always been too clever to break the law, but that was all.

The men he had ruined, the families he had rendered homeless were legion. He followed the voice's instructions carefully. Letting himself out by a little side door, he was able to escape the vigilance of the police or any other watchers. Once round the bend in the road he broke into a run. The air was cool and fresh, the night invigorating. He was lucky to find a last taxi-cab upon the rank, which he commandeered. The man was not anxious for a fare, and consented to take him only part of the distance. Rather than waste time by arguing with the man, Windover accepted the arrangement, and when the man set him down some three minutes' walk from his store he paid him what he demanded without a murmur and hurried on.

On arriving at the store he was very careful to follow to the letter the instructions that had been given him. The great building was in darkness, and the streets were deserted. He saw a policeman standing at the end of the street, but the officer did not notice him, as he was standing in the shadow of the porch. He found his way to the goods entrance, and pressed cautiously at the door. It gave before his pressure, and he stepped inside. The place was dimly lit, and almost immediately a figure stepped out from a nearby doorway. The millionaire made out a stolid-looking man in plain clothes, who touched his hat.

"Mr. Windover, sir?" he said.

"That's right. Am I in time?"

"Hush, sir, if you don't mind." The man laid his finger to his lips. "We don't want to alarm our bird if it can be helped, sir. Inspector Gregson said you would come with me?"

The man spoke so naturally that not for an instant did the financier suspect the trap into which he had fallen.

"Hurry up—I'll follow you," he said, forcing himself to whisper. "I want to see them capture this pest."

"Of course, sir. This way."

The man began to lead the way softly down the long corridors into one of the storerooms. The place was quite dark, and the two men found their way by aid of the "plainclothes man's" torch. Great white shapes of mighty refrigerators loomed about them, vast freezing cupboards which shopkeepers used to store their perishable goods, all worked by electricity. The little circle of light made by the torch flickered from one shape to another. The financier kept close to his guide. Something of the ghostliness of his surroundings had made an impression even upon his mind.

"I can't hear anything," he muttered. "Do you think—"

A sudden ejaculation of horror from his guide silenced him, and he started forward. With a wavering hand the man was holding the torch, whose beams lit up the interior of a vast open refrigerator intended for the storage of whole carcasses of beef. Lying upon the polished surface lay a single red rosebud. Just for an instant the financier did not grasp the significance of the blossom.

"I'm not going any further," said the man at his heels. "Too creepy for me."

THE DARINGS OF THE RED ROSE

Windover laughed. "Don't be a fool," he commanded. "I'm not afraid of any crook. You're a disgrace to the Force. I shall report you."

He strode forward and stooped to pick up the flower. At that instant the utterly unexpected happened. The man behind him leapt upon his shoulders, forcing him into the refrigerator. Then, while he lay sprawling, the great iron door swung to on top of him, and he realised with an overwhelming sense of horror, the trap into which he had fallen.

Face to Face

He staggered to his feet. A small window, some six inches square, was provided in the top part of the door to enable the owner to observe the condition of his goods. Through this the helpless financier peered. An extraordinary sight met his eyes. The room had been lighted with a single lamp, the beams of which were concentrated upon a slim figure clad in black from head to foot, save for a blood-red scarf of some flimsy material wrapped about the lower half of her face. Her eyes, clear, blue, and penetrating, were fixed upon the little window through which he peered.

She began to speak, and he found that he could hear her quite plainly. A small ventilator in the lower part of the cabinet had been left open, and the sound reached him easily. Never to his dying day did the millionaire forget the sound of that quiet, well-modulated voice, impregnated with a hatred so deadly that he quivered before it. Little did he dream that the terrifying apparition before him was a girl well known in society, a girl to whom he had often schemed in vain to be introduced at fashionable parties.

"Windover," began the voice, "I gave you your chance. You had only to pay back voluntarily that which you stole from the unfortunate Wellsiders, and this would never have happened to you. But you refused to be warned. You have deliberately ignored my offer."

Windover laughed. Although a prisoner, some of his courage was returning. He told himself he would never be afraid of a woman. She could keep him there all night if she liked, he decided, but she would get no money out of him.

"I'm afraid you're going to be disappointed," he said. "The money I made out of Wellside I made out of fools. They deserved to lose."

Betty silenced him. "They trusted you," she said, "they trusted you and you betrayed their trust. You robbed them."

Windover shrugged his shoulders. "You can go on talking all night," he said, "but you'll hardly alter my opinion on that point. You may have had a certain amount of success with my colleagues, young lady, if you really are the Red Rose, but you've come up against a very difficult person to tackle this time, I can assure you."

To his surprise the blue eyes that until now had regarded him with an intensity of loathing began to smile, and the voice which had been so menacing became very soft.

"Oh, Mr. Windover," it said, "do you really think so?"

For a full minute he stared at her through the tiny thick glass window, wondering at the curiously unpleasant undertone there had been in that soft voice. And then the terrible truth dawned upon him. He was becoming very

THE DARINGS OF THE RED ROSE

cold. Fear seized him, and he began to tremble. Of course, he had not thought of it before, these fiends had turned on the current. Unless they had mercy he would freeze.

He clawed at the little window, his voice rising to a frenzied shout. "Let me out, let me out! You're killing me—you're murdering me! Let me out!"

The girl shook her head. "When the Wellsiders cried to you for mercy you gave them none," she said.

The cold was becoming intense. The terrified financier felt himself growing numb.

"Don't kill me, don't kill me," he begged. "I implore you—save me, save me!"

Betty raised her hand, and some unseen person in the darkness switched off the current. As the millionaire felt the reviving heat running through his veins his old cunning returned.

"What do you want?" he demanded.

The blue eyes met his squarely through the small patch of glass, which for all his efforts he had not been able to break.

"You know what I want." Betty's voice was very grim. "The money you stole from Wellside."

"You shall have a cheque," he promised.

She laughed at him. "Your bankers have been told to dishonour any drafts made out to the Wellside Fund," she said. "You shouldn't give me credit for being such a fool, Mr. Windover."

The millionaire was puzzled. "What can I give you? You don't think I carry vast sums of money about with me, do you?" he demanded almost angrily.

131

The girl shook her head. "There is one thing you can donate to the Wellside Fund, and that is—" she paused, and added in a whisper—"the black diamond."

The millionaire glanced down at the glittering diamond upon his finger, and his face blackened with fury. "But that's worth a fortune," he expostulated.

"You stole a hundred little fortunes when you ruined Wellside," the girl answered him.

"Never!" The man shook his head. "Never!"

The girl did not answer, but raised her hand, and almost immediately afterwards he felt again the terrifying chill creeping upon him. But to begin with at any rate, his greed and love for his treasure outweighed his fear. The cold became unbearable, and although he strained every nerve to resist it he could not hold out against it. At last, gasping, almost paralysed with the cold, he wrenched the ring from his finger and held it up against the glass. Betty's voice, faint and far away, came to him.

"I shall open the larger ventilator. Push the ring through."

The larger ventilator opened. He huddled towards it, hoping vainly for some warmth from without that would enable him to keep the jewel a little longer, but it was no use, and, finally, he thrust the glittering gem through the slats. They were closed instantly, and again the reviving currents of warm air entered his prison. He pressed his face to the window.

"You've got what you wanted. Let me out," he cried.

There was no answer. All light in the room without had vanished. Suddenly a voice reached him in the darkness.

THE DARINGS OF THE RED ROSE

"I'm afraid you must stay here until the cleaners arrive tomorrow, or your night-watchman recovers consciousness, Mr. Windover," said the girl. "I'm so sorry I've had to treat you like this, but really there seemed no other way of getting you to meet your obligations. Goodnight, Mr. Windover."

All through the small hours the millionaire raved, but it was no use. By the time he was rescued and the extraordinary outrage had been reported in all the papers the mysterious Red Rose had dropped her identity and lay sleeping peacefully, the little red notebook beneath her pillow. The precious jewel was meanwhile safely on board an aeroplane on its way to Amsterdam, where a discreet agent would convert it into a more easily negotiable donation to the Wellside Fund.

EPISODE 8
HER DAY OF RECKONING

Betty Connolly sat at the little writing-desk in her room and rested her chin upon one delicate hand. Marie knelt upon the hearthrug at her side, her face pale and strained.

"The last name," said Betty softly. "This time, Marie, things are going to be very difficult."

The girl who had been her assistant and devoted friend through all the daring adventures of the past months looked up and nodded.

"It seems impossible, Miss Betty," she said. "I know it's no good trying to dissuade you so I won't waste my time. But I feel you're taking a tremendous risk. Scotland Yard is angry now; they have been baulked so often that they are on their mettle. They want the Red Rose, and they'll do everything in their power to capture her."

Betty nodded ruefully. "You're right, Marie," she said. "But the name of Luke Drayton is on the list. Until there is a tick against his name, until he has been forced to contribute towards the resurrection of the town he helped to ruin, my work will not be finished, and I shall not be satisfied."

Marie smiled faintly. "I knew you'd say that, Miss Betty," she said. "All the same, I wish you had taken my advice and not sent him the usual warning. That will put him on his guard, and Scotland yard on the alert."

Betty sighed. "It was a pity," she said, "but it couldn't be helped. Before I took the thing on I made up my mind that each man should have his fair warning, so that if he contributed to the Wellside Fund without pressure I should not subject him to force. So, you see, I had to send the warning to him, Marie."

The other girl frowned, and her dark eyes were rebellious.

"You've played too fair with them all along," she said, "risking your life, to say nothing of your happiness. What about Mr. Kempis, Miss Betty?"

For a moment the other girl turned her face away.

"Don't talk about him, Marie," she said softly; "I can't bear it. That's the one thing that makes me waver in my plan. But I mustn't let it influence me. I have sworn to make Luke Drayton pay, and pay he shall."

Marie shrugged her shoulders.

"How are you going to tackle him? How are you going to evade the police surrounding his house and office?"

Betty hesitated for a moment. Then she got up and paced up and down the room with a slow, purposeful stride.

"Marie," she began slowly, "you think I've been wasting my time these last three weeks, don't you? Running round to parties with people I didn't much care for, cultivating the sort of people who are not usually considered desirable?"

Marie reddened. "Well, I did wonder what you were up to," she said.

"I'll tell you." Betty dropped down into a chair and leant forward, an earnest expression upon her beautiful face.

THE DARINGS OF THE RED ROSE

"I've been making enquiries—all sorts of enquiries—in most unlikely places about this man, Luke Drayton. You see, I saw from the very beginning that the person to protect me from the police in his case was Drayton himself, and I knew that that was only possible if he was protecting himself at the same time.

"I'll explain," she went on as Marie looked mystified. "I had suspected for some time that Luke Drayton had a secret, and I was right. Do you know who he is, Marie? He is the most important 'fence' in all Europe. That is to say, he's a receiver of stolen goods, and I've discovered how he does it. He keeps his own house and business entirely free from visitors who might be recognised by the police as suspicious characters, so he is allowed to go his own way entirely unsuspected.

"How he manages it is this," she went on, lowering her voice. "He flies to France and back every now and again. He does not use his own aeroplane, but hires one from one of the many aerodromes on the east coast. He goes in disguise, spends an hour or so in a little village inland from Boulogne, where he meets his 'clients,' and the deal is made. He pays for the stolen jewels—they are nearly always diamonds—in English gold, which he takes with him. You can always get gold at the banks, you know, if you demand it. Then he flies back again with the jewels which he has bought, and no one is any the wiser."

Marie gasped. "But, Miss Betty, how did you discover all this?"

Betty smiled enigmatically. "It would take too long to tell, Marie," she said. "I've been working hard. I'm playing a risky game, Marie, but I'm not afraid, and something tells me I'm going to succeed."

Marie leant forward. "What are you going to do?"

For a moment Betty seemed to waver, making up her mind whether she were going to confide in Marie or not. Then she pointed to a copy of a French newspaper lying upon the couch.

"That paper is full of a daring robbery in a Paris flat. The Countess D'Oriole has lost a diamond necklace valued at—in English money—about fifty thousand pounds. And something tells me that those diamonds will find their way into Luke Drayton's possession. I had it upon valuable authority that Drayton drew out twenty-five thousand pounds worth of gold. It was an enormous sum, and there was a little gossip about it."

She hesitated and looked at Marie. "Do you see what I'm driving at? A fence usually pays the thieves half the value of the stolen goods. That is just about the sum he would need to buy the Countess's necklace. And it has occurred to me, Marie, that that money would be much better employed in the Wellside Fund than in paying the thieves who robbed the Countess. I suppose you realise that I got my pilot's certificate last week?"

Like a lot of society girls, Betty had taken up flying while the craze was at its height.

"Miss Betty," Marie began, "you're not—you're not—"

Betty laid a finger upon her lips. "I'm going to give Scotland Yard a run for their money," she said softly.

THE DARINGS OF THE RED ROSE

In the Small Hours

It was a little after midnight when a small blue sports car pulled up at the crossroads a mile away from Luke Drayton's country mansion. A slender figure in a leather flying suit climbed out and stood for some moments by the car, her ears strained. It was Betty.

She knew exactly how great a risk she ran in coming upon the errand herself. Scotland Yard knew that Luke Drayton had received the warning of the Red Rose, and were, therefore, on the qui-vive.

Far in the distance she could just hear the throbbing of a motor cycle engine. Her spirits rose. She dimmed her lights, and stood back in the shadow of the hedge. Presently the motor cycle appeared, its headlights throwing up the crossroads in a sudden glare. The rider dismounted and stood for some seconds as though peering at the signpost, and then he whistled softly three times. Betty answered the whistle and stepped forward. The man was her own chauffeur. Three weeks before she had "dismissed" him, and by aid of Lady Derry's references he had obtained a post in Luke Drayton's household. He greeted her eagerly.

"You were right, Miss Betty," he said in a hoarse whisper, "dead right. He's making arrangements to fly to France early to-morrow morning. I was with him when he drove down and made the appointment with the pilot at the aerodrome here. He's going to set out as soon as it's light. That will be about three o'clock. I tell you, Miss Betty, I don't think you'll have a chance of tackling him before he leaves the ground. He's frightened to death of the Red

Rose. The hall's full of plainclothes men, and he's got Mr. Kempis with him."

"They know he's flying early this morning?" said Betty quickly, doing her best to hide the shock which the man's last announcement had been to her.

"Of course. Why should he hide it from them? He says he's going to Manchester. He's a cool customer. He tells the police half the truth, and so there's no reason for them to suspect him. Mr. Kempis will probably drive down to the hangar with him."

Betty shuddered. Things were turning out worse than she imagined, but she still stuck doggedly to her game.

"Look here, Jim," she said. "I want you to drive down to the hangar and tell the shed mechanics and the pilot that Mr. Drayton has changed his mind and will not be travelling this morning. There's no reason why they shouldn't believe you. The moment you're sure that they've taken your message seriously get on your motor bike and go back to the hall. When Mr. Drayton and Mr. Kempis are ready bring them down to the common land two miles on the other side of the aerodrome. You can explain to them that the landing ground by the hangar is obstructed by an injured 'plane. I will be waiting on the common land in my new two-seater Moth. Mr. Kempis hasn't seen it yet, so there's no danger there. The registration marks aren't on it either, and I ought not to be using it really."

The man stared at her. "It's a terrible risk, Miss Betty," he murmured.

Betty shrugged her shoulders and strove to speak lightly. "I can't help that, Jim," she said. "I didn't dream that Mr.

THE DARINGS OF THE RED ROSE

Kempis might be with Drayton. But we must hope for the best. What you've got to do is to hurry Drayton into the 'plane, swing the propeller, and get clear as fast as you can. I shan't stir from the cockpit, and he mustn't get a chance to make me talk. They'll only see my head and shoulders, and I shall have on big goggles and a helmet, while the light will be bad. There's every chance that we get away with it."

She held out her hand. "Goodbye, Jim. All the best—good luck."

The man took it eagerly. "You're a wonder," he said admiringly, "there's no mistake about that."

Then he climbed upon his motor cycle and rode off towards the aerodrome, while Betty returned to her car, and sped off down the road to the private hangar where her own 'plane was awaiting her.

The Parachute Descent

It was a cold, grey dawn, barely light, when Tommy Kempis leant back in the car beside Luke Drayton and glanced curiously at his companion. Jim, the coat collar of his uniform turned up, sat outside the great limousine and drove carefully. So far everything had gone well. His employer had accepted the change of starting ground without demur, and the first stage in the adventure had begun.

Tommy, leaning back among the cushions, wondered idly to himself why the Red Rose always seemed to choose such peculiarly unpleasant specimens for her victims. No one in their wildest dreams could have called Luke Drayton a pleasant person. He was a stocky, middle-sized man with iron-grey hair and a peculiarly vindictive expression upon his hard, unprepossessing face. His eyes were narrow, and never seemed at rest.

He was very quiet, on his guard, but at the moment much more alarmed by the police amateur at his side than by the Red Rose, whose threatening letter had put him into such a panic that he had reported the matter to Scotland Yard.

Just now he was angry with himself for having called in the police at all. Of course, he had not known that his friends on the Continent would choose this particular week to pull off one of their most daring coups, and so send him off on his delicate mission under the very nose of the police. However, he flattered himself that he was not even remotely suspected of anything but the most innocent of business journeys, and he was not particularly alarmed.

However, he was very glad to see a 'plane waiting for him on the broad strip of common, its silver wings glinting in the first rays of morning. He was in flying costume, and it was with some impatience that he permitted his chauffeur to strap him into his parachute. He was anxious to be off, particularly anxious for the Scotland Yard amateur not to have any word with the pilot, wherein he might discover the destination of the 'plane. He said goodbye somewhat hurriedly to Tommy, therefore, and almost ran over to the waiting aeroplane, while Jim darted forward to swing the propeller.

Tommy climbed leisurely out of the car. He could just see the pilot's head, goggled and helmetted, peering out of the cockpit of the machine. Just for a moment it struck him that there was something familiar in the shape of that head,

THE DARINGS OF THE RED ROSE

and the way it was set upon the shoulders, but he had no opportunity to step forward and ascertain if the pilot were a stranger or no, for Drayton was already in the passenger cockpit behind the pilot, and the chauffeur had swung the propeller. With a roar the 'plane was off, taxiing over the short turf like some great unwieldy bird. He stood back and watched it as it rose slowly up into the air, mounting higher and higher until it was but a speck in the distance.

Once up in the early morning air some of Betty's waning courage returned. She had never before experienced such a bad five minutes as she had done when she saw Tommy climb out of the limousine and saunter across the turf towards the 'plane. It was only her passenger's own guilty conscience which had saved her from exposure, she felt sure. She climbed higher and higher, until at a safe altitude she felt that the moment had come.

The only way of communicating in a small aeroplane is by passing notes backwards and forwards across the two cockpits. She turned slightly, and thrust an envelope at her passenger. He took it with some surprise and tore it open. The next moment every drain of colour had vanished from his face, and his thickly gloved hands shook. Out of the envelope had fallen a red rosebud. The note accompanying it was short but explicit.

"The reason for your journey is known to me. I know also that you have with you a large sum of money to pay for the Countess D'Oriole's diamonds. There are two courses open to you. You will either make a parachute descent, leaving the money in the 'plane, whence it will be conveyed to the Wellside Fund, or I shall make a descent myself, leaving you and the machine to crash. To prevent your escaping by parachute it would be my regrettable duty to shoot you first. Any attempt to attack me will result in us both going to perdition together. Take my advice and choose the former course. It is really the only thing you can do. You had your chance to subscribe to the Wellside Fund, and you disdained it. This is your last chance. I give you five minutes."

The paper fluttered out of the fence's nerveless fingers. He tried to shout but the noise of the engine drowned his voice. He dared not touch the figure in front of him lest, as the Red Rose had predicted, they would both crash together. Far below the countryside spread out like a green and yellow patchwork quilt. He felt sick, terrified. But he was an obstinate man, and would not give up his money lightly. He seemed to shrink down further into the cockpit. Near his feet he could feel the suitcase which contained his money. He carried no revolver himself or, he felt, he might have made a stand.

Betty waited for five minutes, and then very deliberately she set the controls, and began to climb to her feet. The parachute strapped to her seemed to fix the man's attention. He tried to struggle forward. Betty turned, and drew something small and gleaming from her overalls.

Drayton, who had caused untold suffering in his time without turning a hair, screamed. He signalled to her feverishly, and scrambled up in his place. The 'plane rocked dangerously. Gripping the ring of his parachute he threw one leg over the side and jumped. Betty just had time to regain her seat and steady the machine. Far below her she caught a glimpse of the parachute, gliding slowly to earth, Drayton hanging like a stone beneath it.

THE DARINGS OF THE RED ROSE

The girl turned the nose of the machine and raced back for London and her private hangar. Her 'plane was like thousands of others; Jim would have made his escape; the Red Rose had performed her last coup, and no one was to know that Miss Betty Connolly had not taken it into her head to take an early morning spin in her new machine. Besides, all things considered, it was hardly likely that Drayton would care to raise too many questions about the twenty-five thousand pounds in gold which he had been forced to contribute to the upkeep of the town he had ruined.

The Last of the Red Rose

The Honourable Tommy Kempis sank back into the little silk-covered armchair in Betty's boudoir and looked at the girl in front of him. It was eleven o'clock in the morning, but there was no sign of weariness on Betty's young face, no hint of the adventures of the small hours. She looked cool and charming in a sleeveless frock of almost green silk, her dark hair bound low at the nape of her neck.

Tommy, on the other hand, appeared to be unusually dejected.

"Betty," he said, "I'm giving up my amateur sleuthing. I haven't got the temperament. And not only am I not successful, but I can't get up any sympathy for my elusive crook's victims. Why don't you marry me, and we'll go off on a glorious honeymoon somewhere where the Red Rose has never been heard of?"

Betty looked at him wistfully, but she did not answer, and presently he rose to his feet, and came towards her.

"My dear," he said, looking down at her, "I wish you'd take me seriously. I admit I'm not much good as a detective, but I'd make a wonderful husband."

Still she did not answer, and he, thinking that the subject embarrassed her, changed it hurriedly.

"D'you know why I've resigned from this Red Rose business?" he said. "Because I'm licked—because we're all licked. The Red Rose is too clever for us. At three o'clock this morning I saw Luke Drayton, the last person who received the Red Rose's warning, off to Manchester on an aeroplane. At half-past eight this morning he was discovered wandering about in a Kentish field ten miles from anywhere, and wild horses won't drag from him what happened. He seemed to have made his descent by parachute, and that was all he would tell us. We then discovered that the 'plane he went up in was not the one he chartered, and his chauffeur, who drove him to the mystery 'plane, has disappeared.

"The police are convinced that the Red Rose is at the bottom of it all, but they are powerless to act since Drayton won't make any charge. The Red Rose, whoever she is, has got some hold over him that's keeping him silent. I'm through with the Red Rose. Let her do what else she likes. I shan't be mixed up in the affair."

To his intense surprise, the girl took his hands in hers and looked up into his face.

"I've got to tell you, Tommy," she said. "I can't let you go on loving me without telling the truth. I am the Red Rose. Drayton was a receiver of stolen goods. There was twenty-five thousand pounds in gold in that aeroplane this morning, which he was taking over to buy the Countess

THE DARINGS OF THE RED ROSE

D'Oriole's diamonds from the thieves who had stolen them. I made him jump out of the aeroplane, and the money is now on its way to the Wellside Fund. I do not think Drayton wants police assistance. They might prove dangerous friends."

Tommy was staring at her incredulously.

"You, Betty?" he said. "I can't believe it. It's absurd."

The girl shook her head. "It's true, Tommy, you've got to face it. Oh, my dear, let me tell you my side of the story, let me tell you why."

With her eyes on his and her lips trembling she poured out her whole story of Wellside and of her oath. The young man listened gravely, his eyes fixed upon her face. At last her passionate recital came to an end.

The young man moved towards her, and before she realised what had happened his arms were about her and he was holding her close to him.

"Oh, Betty," he said. "My wonderful, brave little Betty! I understand—of course, I do! You'll marry me now?"

Betty raised her lips to his. "Yes," she whispered.

THE DARINGS OF THE RED ROSE

The Darings of the Red Rose by Margery Allingham, originally published anonymously in *Weekly Welcome* in 1930, was first gathered together in book form by Crippen & Landru, Publishers, Norfolk, Virginia, in 1995. The introduction is by B. A. Pike, and the cover design by Deborah Miller. The book was printed and bound by Thomson-Shore, Inc., Dexter, Michigan. The type faces include Garamond Antiqua 12 point for the text, Caslon Open Face 36 point for the capital letters beginning each story, and Bernhard Modern for the title page, running titles, and page numerals. The paper stock is 60 pound Glatfelter Supple Opaque. Eight-hundred and fifty copies comprise the first edition. *The Darings of the Red Rose* was published on October 15, 1995.

CRIPPEN & LANDRU, PUBLISHERS
Post Office Box 9315
Norfolk, Virginia 23505-9315
USA

Crippen & Landru publishes first editions of important works by detective and mystery writers, specializing in short-story collections. Each book contains a new introduction by the author or by a recognized expert in the field. Books by living authors will be available in signed and numbered editions, and the number of copies printed in both trade and limited versions will be recorded in a colophon at the end of each volume. Crippen & Landru books are produced under the supervision of Douglas G. Greene.

The following books are now (October 1995) available or forthcoming:

SPEAK OF THE DEVIL
By John Dickson Carr
Introduction by Tony Medawar

The master of the locked-room mystery tells the story of the ghostly manifestations of a woman hanged for murder. Swordplay, derring-do, and fairplay puzzling take place in the England of 1816. Originally broadcast in 8 parts on BBC-radio in 1941, this long-lost mystery combines eerie atmosphere and crimes that are only too real. *Ellery Queen's Mystery Magazine* reviewed the book as "suspenseful and masterfully constructed," and *Mystery Scene* wrote, "whatever else Crippen & Landru may offer, this first title justifies its existence." Cover by Deborah Miller. Trade paperback (ISBN: 1-885941-00-5) $12.95.

THE McCONE FILES
By Marcia Muller
Introduction by the Author

The contemporary female private eye story began in 1977 when Edgar-nominee Marcia Muller published *Edwin of the Iron Shoes*, about Sharon McCone, investigator for the All Souls legal co-op. One of the most humane and sympathetic of all current sleuths, McCone investigates cases which make a difference not only to her clients but to the world about her. *The McCone Files* contains the thirteen previously published short stories about McCone as well as two written specially for this volume. *Ellery Queen's Mystery Magazine* wrote, "Of the leading triumvirate of female private-eye authors . . . , Muller is the most skilled at the short story form, offering fully-plotted puzzles and a real feel for The City." Cover by Carol Heyer. Signed, limited clothbound edition, out of print. Trade paperback (ISBN: 1-885941-04-6) $15.00.

DIAGNOSIS: IMPOSSIBLE
THE PROBLEMS OF DR. SAM HAWTHORNE
By Edward D. Hoch
Introduction by the Author

"Satan himself would be proud of his ingenuity," John Dickson Carr said of Edward D. Hoch, today's major exponent of the Challenge-to-the-Reader detective story. The former President of the Mystery Writers of America and an Edgar-Award winner, Hoch is author of many classics featuring New England country doctor Sam Hawthorne, who in the 1920s and 1930s specialized in locked rooms and other impossible crimes. *Diagnosis: Impossible* begins with the tale of a horse-and-buggy that vanishes inside a covered bridge and continues with nine other ingenious and atmospheric stories. Cover by Carol Heyer. Forthcoming in signed, limited clothbound edition (ISBN: 1-885941-03-X) and in trade paperback (ISBN: 1-885941-02-1).

SPADEWORK
By Bill Pronzini
Introduction by Marcia Muller

The recipient of The Eye for Lifetime Achievement from the Private Eye Writers of America, Bill Pronzini is one of the grandmasters of the detective fiction, and his Nameless private investigator continues the Hammett-Chandler-Macdonald tradition of lone investigators down Mean Streets. Yet Nameless has never succumbed to the world-weary cynicism of too many fictional sleuths, nor the penchant to shoot before thinking, and his cases are filled with twists, turns, and solid clueing. *Spadework* contains all of his previously uncollected short cases. Cover by Carol Heyer. Forthcoming in signed, limited clothbound edition (ISBN: 1-885941-03-X) and in trade paperback (ISBN: 1-885941-02-1).

Crippen & Landru offers discounts to individuals and institutions who place standing orders for its publications.